# A BANDIT'S TALE

ALSO BY
DEBORAH HOPKINSON

*The Great Trouble:
A Mystery of London,
the Blue Death,
and a Boy Called Eel*

*Into the Firestorm:
A Novel of San Francisco,
1906*

# A BANDIT'S TALE

## THE MUDDLED MISADVENTURES OF A PICKPOCKET

Deborah Hopkinson

Alfred A. Knopf

*New York*

THIS IS A BORZOI BOOK PUBLISHED BY ALFRED A. KNOPF

For picture credits, please see page 287.

Visit us on the Web! randomhousekids.com

Educators and librarians, for a variety of teaching tools, visit us at RHTeachersLibrarians.com

*Library of Congress Cataloging-in-Publication Data*
Hopkinson, Deborah.
A bandit's tale : the muddled misadventures of a pickpocket / Deborah Hopkinson. — First edition.
pages ; cm.
Summary: In March of 1887, Rocco, an eleven-year-old from an Italian village, arrives in New York City, where he is forced to live in squalor and beg for money as a street musician, but he finds the city's cruelty to children and animals intolerable and sets out to make things better, whatever the cost to himself.
ISBN 978-0-385-75499-6 (trade) — ISBN 978-0-385-75500-9 (lib. bdg.) — ISBN 978-0-385-75501-6 (ebook)
[1. Conduct of life—Fiction. 2. Child labor—Fiction. 3. Child abuse—Fiction. 4. Immigrants—New York (State)—New York—Fiction. 5. Italians—New York (State)—New York—Fiction. 6. Animals—Treatment—Fiction. 7. New York (N.Y.)—History—19th century—Fiction.] I. Title.
PZ7.H778125Ban 2016
[Fic]—dc23
2015004491

The text of this book is set in 12-point New Hoefler.

Printed in the United States of America
April 2016
10 9 8 7 6 5 4 3 2 1

First Edition

For Barbara and Jim,
and for Dimitri,
lovers of animals
and New York City

# CONTENTS

## BOOK TWO
*Fall 1887*

Long ago it was said that "one half of the world does not know how the other half lives."

—Jacob Riis, *How the Other Half Lives*

Do you know why this world is as bad as it is? . . . It is because people think only about their own business, and won't trouble themselves to stand up for the oppressed, nor bring the wrongdoer to light. . . . My doctrine is this, that if we see cruelty or wrong that we have the power to stop, and do nothing, we make ourselves sharers in the guilt.

—Anna Sewell, *Black Beauty*

I have counted on one of the lines of this City one hundred persons upon a car, while the snow was eight or ten inches deep. . . . I submit this is a cruel load for any two horses.

—Henry Bergh, letter in the *New York Times,*
December 26, 1871

# PROLOGUE

## Late Winter 1887

*Containing the history of a contract,
with a word or two about a donkey*

All my troubles began with a donkey. If it hadn't been
for one obstinate, bad-tempered beast, my parents
wouldn't have rented me out to a stranger for twenty
dollars a year.

I can name a few men (you'll meet them in the course
of this history) who would swear Papa and Mama were
well rid of a lying rascal like me. But I hope you'll make
up your own mind once you hear my tale.

The deal was made on a night so still every sound
startled like a slap. I was half asleep when I heard heavy
steps on the stones outside. Whoever it was limped.
*Clomp, CLOMP. Clomp, CLOMP.* I woke up a little more
then. I knew almost everyone in our village, and no one
walked like this.

When the footsteps halted, I caught the sound of a low, quick rap: the knock of someone who was expected. By now I was curious as a mouse on a shelf stacked with cheese. I untangled my legs from the straw pallet I shared with my brother and sisters and tiptoed to where I could peer into our other room.

As the door swung open, a shadow filled the space like an enormous black cloud. It settled into the shape of a man, who, to my surprise, turned out to be rather short. The stranger lumbered in, dragging his right leg behind him. He lowered himself heavily into the chair Papa pulled out for him at our table. I could hear the rustle of Mama's long black skirt as she bustled to serve him a cup of homemade wine.

"Rocco will be twelve this summer. He might be skinny as a twig, but he's strong," Papa said. "I put a hoe in his hands when he was five, and he's been helping me in the fields ever since."

"Is he a good boy?" the man asked. He took a long swig of wine, then wiped the back of his hand across his mouth. Like me, he was watching Papa, but Mama answered.

"*Sì, sì,* Rocco is a good son," she murmured quickly, rushing to fill his cup again.

Papa said nothing. He couldn't. Even a stranger, I guessed, would already know what Signor Ferri, our landlord and one of the most important men in town, had declared in the piazza that day, loud enough for all ears to hear.

"I have something to say, men. As you know, I gave Signor Zaccaro's son Rocco a post of honor, caring for the donkeys and mules I rent to you all," Signor Ferri had announced, standing in front of the farmers before they headed down the mountain to the fields.

Signor Ferri was so rich his wife had even bought a piano, the only one in town. Its arrival was like a festival procession. We paraded behind the mule-drawn cart to the landlord's house at the very top of Calvello. My little sister, Emilia, was so fascinated by the piano she sometimes followed me when I worked in the landlord's stable just so she could stand in the yard and hear Signora Ferri practice.

"This ungrateful boy has abused my trust and stolen from me. Rocco Zaccaro is no longer to step foot anywhere near my home," the landlord said. "It would be best not to let your children have anything to do with him."

Then the landlord fixed his cold, dark eyes on me. "That boy is a bandit."


I shook my head, as if to sweep the memory away. It was useless. I could never forget my father's look of shame as he stood with bowed head, stared at and pitied by his neighbors. It is a hard thing indeed when the elder son brings dishonor on the family name.

Now I tried to make out what the stranger was saying. He was speaking quickly, using his hands to paint pictures in the air. I caught the word "America."

That's when I knew. I wanted to rush out and beg, *No! Don't send me away, Papa. I'm sorry. I can explain. It's not what you think.*

I said nothing, but I must have let out a little gasp, because all three turned my way. Mama looked at me, her eyes already filling with tears.

One glance at Papa's face told me the deal was already done. "Rocco, come here."

No matter what they said about America and the good chance it would be for me, I knew it wasn't really about that. This was a punishment.

# BOOK ONE

*Spring 1887*

# CHAPTER 1

*In which my (mis)adventures begin
and many tearful goodbyes are said*

These days, when anyone asks, I say I'm an American, New York City–born. And why not? Because, in a way, I *was* born here.

Right here, smack in the middle of this giant, swarming bees' nest of a place, is where I became me: Rocco Zaccaro, pickpocket, liar extraordinaire, and escaped convict, among other things. I'm a true guttersnipe—a scruffy and badly behaved street kid. I'm an alley rat of Mulberry Bend and Bandits' Roost.

And though it may not be exactly correct to say I was born in New York City, well, I ask you: Just what *is* truth? My adventures have taught me that truth isn't a solid thing, like a brick you can heft in your hand. Naw, it's more like a shadow that changes shape depending on the time of day. Your shadow looks one way in the morning, another in late afternoon. At noon on a sunny day? It just about disappears. But it's still your shadow.

Nonetheless, I'm guessing you *do* want to know some facts—basic, hard facts—so you can make up your mind about me. Am I a poor, misfortunate victim, whose parents sold him to a wicked villain? Or am I a young scoundrel, who deserves every bad turn that has come his way? Well, as I said at the beginning, you'll have to decide that for yourself. All I ask is that you keep an open mind.

As for those facts, I arrived in New York City in March 1887 at the age of eleven, plucked from the region in southern Italy we call Basilicata, province of Potenza, hill town of Calvello, a desperately poor place, where peasants like my parents struggled to survive.

It's also a fact that Mama named me Rocco because I was born on August 16, feast day of Saint Rocco, patron saint of the sick, dogs, and falsely accused people.

Mama said that Rocco was a rich man from Montpellier, France, who gave up his fortune to go on pilgrimage. While caring for others during an epidemic, Rocco fell ill. He was exiled to the forest, where a dog— and the dog's noble owner—befriended him and nursed him back to health. But when Rocco finally returned home, he was falsely accused of being a spy and put in jail, where he stayed for five years, until he died. Whew! Quite a story, don't you think?

Mama told me that statues of Rocco often show him

with a dog. I've never had a dog myself. However, as you will discover later in this history, I have met a man who, like the saint himself, was befriended by a kindly canine. As for Saint Rocco being the patron of the falsely accused, well, I'll have more to say about that later too.

Calvello is like no place you'll find in America. Our village is perched on the side of a steep, jutting hill, which actually looks a bit like a molehill sticking up from the pastures and fields below. As for the town itself, it's no more than a jumble of limestone dwellings, all huddled next to one another like pigeons in a storm.

Each May, families would celebrate the festival of the Madonna del Monte Saraceno, honoring the Virgin Mary with songs and a procession that wound through the streets.

Come fall, we'd trail Mama like little chicks as we combed the forest for chestnuts: *le castagne*. Anna and Emilia and I would kick the leaves away, searching for the fallen treasure hidden beneath, with little Vito toddling behind us on his chubby legs. Chestnuts have spiky burrs, and it took days to pick them out of our skin. We didn't mind—the taste of roasted chestnuts was worth it.

But everyday life was hard. Children in Calvello didn't go to school beyond age eight or nine. We were needed to help our parents. Sometimes, when we were supposed to be asleep, I'd hear Mama and Papa talking anxiously, their voices sharp as those stinging prickles. They worried about paying rent in the form of grain to Signor Ferri. Mama fretted about having enough food to get through the winter.

We kept a goat, plus a few sheep and pigs. We tried to slaughter at least one pig each winter so Mama could make sausages. She spiced them with wild fennel and hung them from the rafters to dry.

We'd had our own donkey once, but poor crops and high taxes had forced Papa to sell it. Now Signor Ferri owned the only donkeys and mules in town, renting them out to Papa and the other peasants when there was a need to carry heavy loads. At ten, in addition to helping in the fields, I'd gotten an extra job working in the landlord's stable—the very job I'd lost in that public, shameful way.

All in all, our family's prospects were bleak when the stranger Giovanni Ancarola appeared in our midst, spinning a story bright as gold. Even if I hadn't embarrassed Papa, his proposition would have been hard for my parents to pass up. Signor Ancarola was a padrone—a boss man and patron—who held out a promise, a chance for things to be different someday.

Best of all, the padrone offered cash. Under the contract, Signor Ancarola would get me, a string bean of a boy (and a disgrace besides), and be my master. My parents would receive an amount equal to twenty American dollars each year for the next four years, so long as I kept working for him in America. Not only that, but there'd be one less mouth to feed with me gone.

Two days from that fateful night, Giovanni Ancarola returned to take me away. To my astonishment, he had Old Biter with him.

"Where'd you get that donkey?" I blurted out.

"Like him, do you?" Signor Ancarola grinned. "Signor Ferri sold him to me. He said you were good with donkeys, and you'd especially know how to handle this one."

I swallowed hard and felt my heart race with anger. That's when I realized how the padrone had chosen me: The landlord had sent him to our door. Signor Ferri wanted me gone from his village.

And I knew exactly why.

Signor Ancarola went inside to finish his business with Papa, leaving me holding Old Biter's rope. Six-year-old Emilia tried to hug me one more time, without getting too close to the donkey. Tears ran down her cheeks.

But Anna, the oldest of us at thirteen, and the boldest too, peered at me with dry eyes. Anna wouldn't have been frightened the way I was; she wouldn't have tossed and turned all night, imagining gigantic waves swallowing her on the passage.

Anna grasped my free hand with both of hers, pressing a pair of knit socks into it. She was clever, good at knitting, at cooking, at everything she did. Leaning forward, she whispered urgently, "Come back for us someday, Rocco. Come back for *me*."

I nodded, but that wasn't good enough for her. Anna squeezed my hand so hard it hurt. "You must promise. Will you do that, little brother?"

"*Sì,* I promise," I croaked.

Papa and the padrone emerged into the sunshine. The padrone took the donkey's rope from me and said, "Time to go, Rocco. You will do fine—if you listen and follow the rules."

He started off, leaving my family huddled in our doorway. I began to follow, then Vito started wailing, "Rocco, Rocco!"

I ran back and hugged Anna and Emilia. Even Anna was crying now. I swept up little Vito, who wrapped himself, spider-like, around my neck. He was only two, and as I tickled his warm belly, I wondered if he would even remember me.

Mama folded me in her thin, strong arms. "I'll pray to the saints for you. Saint Rocco will keep you well." That was always her biggest fear: that we would get sick.

I gave Papa a quick hug. He kept his face a mask. I almost whispered the truth then, all of it. But I swallowed the words. I had made a promise. Besides, it was too late.

I looked back once before we turned the corner, half hoping Papa would change his mind and call me back. He was patting his pocket, probably already thinking about the money. If he had other feelings, they were buried much deeper than a pocket.

A few streets away, we stopped to pick up two other boys. They were pathetic-looking creatures, ten-year-old cousins who didn't seem strong enough to walk to Naples, more than a hundred miles away, let alone embark on a perilous boat trip across a stormy ocean.

I didn't know them well. Their mothers were twins, which might be why I had trouble telling them apart at first. They had shaggy black hair and dark round eyes. Marco was slight, Luigi slender as a reed.

"Call me Padrone. If anyone asks, I'm your uncle," Padrone told us. He would repeat this instruction many times.

"You don't look like us," I murmured under my breath, though I knew it was a mistake as soon as it was out.

Ever since I can remember, Mama had warned me about speaking without thinking first. "Your words shouldn't rush out of you like a hasty stream," she would say. "You must try to be more like Papa."

I understood what she meant; I just had a hard time doing it. Often, as soon as a thought dropped into my head, it popped out of my mouth.

Padrone did not appreciate my comment. He gave me a quick cuff on the side of my head. "When I give you orders, you don't talk back. That goes for all of you. Understand?"

*"Sì, sì, signore,"* we all chimed in unison.

"Here, Rocco," said Signor Ancarola, tossing the donkey's rope to me. "Take charge of your friend."

And so we set out.

# CHAPTER 2

*Giving an account of a dusty journey by foot;
another goodbye*

Marco and Luigi wouldn't stop crying. It was plain to see they'd never left home before. Their parents must have been desperate, because the two had the look of chicks pushed out of the nest too soon. Snot dripped from their noses. Rivulets of grimy tears stained their cheeks.

In short, it was disgusting.

"Wipe your noses," I hissed as we snaked down to the valley floor. "Stay behind the donkey and stop sniveling. No one wants to hear you."

Without a word of protest, they did exactly as I ordered, falling silently into place behind Old Biter like pocket-sized soldiers heading off to war. I was glad. If they'd kept up their whimpering and sniffling, I was afraid I might start too. Their tears reminded me that every mile took me away from the only home I had.

Still, even on that first, bewildering day, as each twist and turn of a dusty mule path brought the sight of something new, I couldn't help feeling a tiny shiver of excitement. I was off on an adventure, even if I was leading a bad-tempered donkey. Who could tell what might happen next?

Now, you might think that even a donkey might also be a little excited, in a donkeyish sort of way, about being on a journey and seeing new things. Well, you would be wrong. In fact, it was as if Old Biter blamed me that he was plodding along a dusty road instead of munching hay contentedly at home.

The night before we'd set off, while I'd tossed and turned with fear about what lay ahead, I'd fingered the scar on my arm. The only good thing about being sent away, I'd decided, was that I'd never have to look at Old Biter's ugly yellow teeth or feel them tear into my flesh again.

And here he was—teeth and all. That spiteful creature lit into me as soon as Padrone called a halt to our first day's walk. I'd begun to unload the bags from his back when he whipped his neck around. In the blink of an eye, he went for my left arm, no doubt hoping to add another half-moon scar to the one he'd already given me.

I should have been more careful, I suppose. I should have talked to him gently and moved more slowly. I was just so tired, inside and out. My feet were sore. My heart was sore. Luckily, I was able to jump back in time to get just a nip, not a bite. I yelped and stamped my feet. I almost kicked him, then thought better of it. Old Biter would definitely kick back.

"I thought you were supposed to know about this beast," said Padrone. "I hope the skin isn't broken. I can't afford for you to get sick from a wound.

"Leave the old boy to me," he added, taking the rope from my hand. "Go collect firewood."

It occurred to me that Giovanni Ancarola might be as vicious as my ill-tempered four-legged friend, but he wouldn't trample us entirely. Marco, Luigi, and I were, after all, valuable property.

Our journey soon settled into a pattern. We followed rugged shepherds' paths and well-worn mule tracks, winding our way up and down hills, through villages, and onto the main road to Naples. Padrone had warned that it might take us at least a week, and that we had no time to lose.

"We will walk all night if we have to," he told us. "We cannot be late."

Luigi and Marco continued to sob themselves to sleep each night, though where they got the energy, I have no idea. Still, they walked—I'll say that for them. We all did, from early light until it was too dark to see. We carried bread, cheese, and water and ate outside, sitting on the ground. On occasion our padrone would plant us outside of a little tavern so he could drink some wine. There was no danger of us running away. Where would we go in a strange town with no friends or family?

Padrone pushed us. It couldn't have been easy with his limp, but he never slowed down. He never mentioned his leg or why it dragged. Whatever else he was, Signor Ancarola wasn't a complainer. Perhaps that was why he couldn't stand grumbling in others. We learned to hold our tongues no matter how hungry or thirsty we were, or how big the ugly blisters blossoming on our feet became.

"Come on, the ship will not wait," Padrone would bark at Luigi whenever he began to lag behind, which was often. Luigi seemed to live in a world of his own, a dreamy place where he might stop for a minute to stare up at a cloud, mouth open, or bend down to count ants in the dirt. Sometimes I wondered if he truly grasped what was happening to him or where we were heading.

Marco understood, though. One night, he asked Signor Ancarola, "What's it like, New York City?"

I was surprised. Marco usually kept to himself. I leaned forward, eager to hear the answer. Padrone only grunted and said, "Big."

It wasn't until we stood on the busy dock in Naples and were about to board the Anchor Line steamship *Elysia* that I also got the nerve to ask a question. It was what I wanted to know most. "Padrone, what will we do in America? What is the business we will help you with?"

You may think it strange I didn't know, but if Papa

knew, he hadn't told me. I waited almost breathlessly for the answer, as if my whole future depended on it. And I suppose in a way it did, for I had begun to form a plan.

It had come to me as I walked, mile after mile. With each step it had grown clearer, almost the way you can walk closer to a tree and begin to make out the pattern of the bark on its trunk. The plan was this: Perhaps going to America might not be a bad thing after all. America might be the answer. There, I could become a work boss like Giovanni Ancarola.

Then, someday, I would return to stand before Papa, triumphant. I'd have a pouch full of coins and shoes so shiny you could see the sky in them. Papa would see that I had become as wealthy and important as Signor Ferri. In an instant, I would wipe out the dishonor I had brought to him.

Papa would meet my eyes, shake my hand, and look at me with pride. He would bring me to the piazza and say to the men, *Here is my son Rocco, back from America, where he has become a prosperous young man.*

Maybe if Anna still wanted to go to America, she and I would set off again, back to the golden land.

As I waited to find out what business held the key to this grand scheme, I was shocked to hear Padrone chortle, a strange, unsettling sound that startled Luigi so much he flinched.

"Didn't your father tell you anything?" he asked. "You're to be a street musician."

"A street musician?" I repeated. "What is that?"

"Just what the words say: You'll play the harp or violin for money on the streets and bring me back your earnings each night."

*Bring him the money? What about money for me?*

"I don't know how to play the harp or the violin," I protested. "Isn't there something else I could do?"

"There is nothing else," he said, picking at his teeth with a twig he'd found on the road. "It's not hard. You only need to know a few songs."

"But—" I began.

"Enough questions," he barked. "If you turn out to be as stupid in America as you are now, I'll give you a triangle to hit. And hit *you* until you've learned it."


Before we depart my native land, I have one more good-bye to relate. The donkey is about to pass out of this story and into one of his own. For on that dock in Naples, Signor Ancarola sold Old Biter to a wrinkled shrimp of a man, an ex-sailor who claimed he'd had enough of the sea and wanted to spend the rest of his days on dry land as a peddler.

I watched the coins change hands, wondering if I should call out a warning to the unsuspecting new owner. Once he had the reins in his callused hands, the sailor leaned over and planted a gigantic kiss almost exactly on the donkey's lips. I nearly gasped, certain that at any second the sailor's disembodied nose would go flying through the air.

"We will be good friends now, *amore mio,* my sweet-heart," the sailor cooed, stepping back a little, a smile on his face as bright as the sun that danced on the sea just beyond where we stood. "Prepare to be pampered like no other donkey in Naples. From now on, I shall call you Little Dove."

I gawked and held my breath. This idiot sailor was in for a sad awakening.

All at once Old Biter shuffled forward until his head rested against the sailor's chest. He sighed deeply and closed his eyes, as though sinking onto a soft pillow at the end of a long day.

I was still on dry land. Yet suddenly I felt all wobbly, as if I was already on a swaying deck. I'd blamed this donkey for what had happened, for ruining my life, for turning me into a castaway. I was convinced Old Biter was as much my enemy as the landlord himself. Now, just for a second, I wasn't sure.

And when the donkey fixed me with one dark eye before turning away, I could almost have sworn that the fiendish beast winked.

# CHAPTER 3

---

*Arrival, after a disagreeable*
*(and often disgusting) crossing*

---

It's not that I don't remember crossing the Atlantic in steerage on that stinking tub of a ship. It's just that I don't want to talk about it. And you should thank me— I'm skipping this for your sake.

For I doubt you wish to hear detailed descriptions of how my stomach turned itself inside out like a sock, not just once but over and over again, until I was so weak I was lying in a soup of my own foul-smelling vomit. Or how, when there was nothing else to eject, I retched up some slimy green bile that must have come from parts of my insides peeling away.

Nor will I subject you to a vivid depiction of my encounters with the rats: enormous, bold, beady-eyed creatures who roamed the ship like they owned it and would have made Old Biter himself turn tail.

So, let's just say I made it. We all did. After what seemed an eternity of misery, we arrived in New York Harbor. Our legs shook when we stepped unsteadily off the *Elysia* at last. That was the first time I heard Luigi laugh.

"Look at me! I can't walk straight," he giggled. He held on to Marco and me, veering giddily as we were bumped along in a crowd of dazed, grateful passengers. Like the rest of us, he was amazed to be on solid ground again and slightly surprised to be alive.

Padrone had done all the talking on board the ship, and he kept on that way, though his English was never very good. He'd already been through Castle Garden, at the southern tip of Manhattan, where immigrants were processed.

Luigi, Marco, and I stood openmouthed in the midst of an enormous circular hall, our ears barraged by voices speaking many languages. "So many people! Are they all staying here in New York?" I asked.

Padrone shook his head. "Some will take trains to other parts of America."

We waited with Padrone in line at the registration desk. Padrone reminded us that he would answer the inspector's questions about who we were.

"Remember, I am your uncle, bringing you to live with family in New York City," he told us.

When we were free to go, we went to the baggage

room for Signor Ancarola's bags. Marco and Luigi had brought nothing; I had only a small pillowcase, which I'd kept with me. Then he hired a cart to take us to our new home. I may as well tell you the address now: 45 Crosby Street, near Broome and Broadway in Lower Manhattan. (The building is still there, by the way, so if you're ever in the neighborhood, you may want to go see it for yourself.)

It wasn't a long ride, but I was soon shivering as we rumbled along. I hadn't realized how much colder it would be here. Being high, Calvello gets cool in winter, but Mama made sure we had plenty of firewood. I'd never felt anything like this biting, badgering wind. As I would soon find out, March is changeable. If you ask me, March doesn't know whether it belongs to winter or spring, so it ends up torn between them, like a bone being fought over by two hungry dogs.

Marco, Luigi, and I huddled together, trying to take in our unfamiliar surroundings. This new place seemed so alive it hummed. Night had just fallen, yet the streets were still busy, full of people hurrying to and fro. Horses drawing cabs and carts sped by us, their iron-shod hooves clanging and clopping.

"It's loud here!" cried Luigi, blocking his ears with his hands.

What would happen to us next? Surely, Signor Ancarola wouldn't send us out into this vast, confusing maze on our own. I shivered some more, only partly from the cold, and even let Luigi tuck himself underneath my arm like a small bird. My teeth chattered. My stomach hurt from tensing my muscles against the wind. The cart turned a corner and bumped along narrow side streets for a while. Then it stopped.

"Here," Padrone grunted.

We scrambled down on stiff legs. Luigi clung to me, and I didn't shake him off. Signor Ancarola led us around to the back of a building, perhaps three stories high. Without knocking, he opened a wooden door. A man appeared with a kerosene lamp. Padrone took it and stepped inside, the three of us close on his heels.

The staircase was dark as a moonless night in Calvello, where everyone went to bed with the sun. I reached out to hold on to something, afraid I might topple into the gloom below. There was no handle to grab, just a clammy, damp wall against my fingers. It felt as if we were descending back into the bowels of the ship. The raw cold was the same, the stench almost as bad.

Our shadows in the lamplight loomed like monsters in the closed space; the shapes reminded me of the evening when the padrone had come to our door. That night had brought me here.

"Sleep there." Padrone gestured to a corner piled with straw. Some dark lumps were scattered in the middle. The lamp caught a foot, a shock of dark hair, a tangle of arms and legs.

"Don't we get a blanket?" I blurted, and got a push instead.

I stumbled over to claim a spot on the edge, leaving Marco and Luigi to try to squeeze in among the other bodies on the straw. Almost at once I realized I'd made a mistake. Luigi and Marco were soon burrowed in, getting at least a little warmth from the others. I shivered. By staying apart, I'd missed my chance at that.

A few minutes later, I heard a soft rustling. At first, I assumed it was rats. Not this time. A shape detached itself from the nest behind me and crept closer. I felt a pawing at the little pillowcase I'd put by my side. The loaf of bread Mama had packed for me was long gone, but I still had one extra shirt and the pair of socks Anna had knit.

I waited, choosing my moment with care. Then I shot up and hissed, "Off!"

The would-be thief gave a low giggle and slunk away. I watched where he went so I could mark him in the morning. Then I put the pillowcase under my head, where it should have been from the beginning. Another mistake I wouldn't make again.

*Only once,* I told myself. *It's all right to make a mistake, but only once.*

The next morning, Padrone banged a spoon on a kettle, startling me out of a fitful dream of being at home with Vito curled next to me. The image slipped away before I was even on my feet, shaking straw out of my hair. I'd been gone several weeks now, and every day my memories of Calvello faded a little. Soon they would be as far away as a wisp of cloud.

I looked around. There were about twenty boys here, filthy and covered with sores. They wore odds and ends of clothes. This was no home, just a vile, rank hovel of a place. I'd kept the landlord's stable cleaner than this. *It smelled a lot better too,* I thought.

I won't be ruining the suspense if I tell you now that 45 Crosby Street would one day (in part thanks to my own courage and daring, I might add) become known throughout the city for exactly what it was: a terrible, notorious "child den," where boys were kept like animals and made to do whatever their masters commanded.

It would be a long time, though, before anyone would see that, and it would take all I had to bring it off. When I arrived, all that went on here and in places like it was invisible to the outside world. Even when we were out on the streets—and we were on those streets day in and day out—no one really saw us.

People looked. They simply didn't see.

We climbed up to the main floor. The windows were covered with old cloths, making the room nearly as dim as the cellar below. There was a small coal stove, a few cupboards, a bare table, and a wooden platform with a mattress, which I supposed was for the padrone. Against one wall, violins and large harps leaned together like tired travelers.

The front of the main floor, facing the street, was a public saloon run by a man named Luigi Careli, who'd been here for years and had a reputation in Little Italy of knowing how to get things done. He was a sort of middleman, giving newcomers from the home country a mailing address to use until they got settled. He also helped immigrants find jobs with his contacts who needed dayworkers. I didn't have any direct dealings with Signor Careli, which was probably just as well. He was a man you wouldn't want to cross.

I soon found out from the other boys that Signor Ancarola rented this half of the main floor, as well as the cellar. Other padroni kept more boys upstairs. Each padrone at 45 Crosby Street controlled his own street musicians. These men were like spiders, with webs that stretched all over Little Italy. Once you were caught in their sticky threads, it was hard to get out.

And I was caught.


That morning, and every morning after, we each got a small bowl of macaroni to eat with our fingers. There was also a hunk of black bread, about three inches square. I had it halfway to my mouth before I decided to stuff it in my pocket for later.

The macaroni was mushy and cold, nothing like what Mama made, which she served hot with spicy tomato sauce and fresh, tangy olive oil. Sometimes she made a stew with onions, peppers, tomatoes, mushrooms, and potatoes, which we ate with warm, crispy bread. My stomach growled just thinking about it.

Back in Calvello, though we didn't have much, at least what we ate was fresh. Our clothes smelled like sunshine after Mama hung them to dry. The boys around me now were foul-smelling and covered with grime. I wondered if any of them ever took baths. Not very often, I guessed.

Now I was one of them, along with Marco and Luigi. I would soon smell as disgusting as the rest, be just as itchy from flea bites and lice. I heard someone cough, a horrible wracking sound. I hoped Mama wouldn't give up praying to Saint Rocco. I might need his protection to stay alive.

I took it all in, then made a quick decision. I walked up to Giovanni Ancarola, who had gone over to the instruments, ready to begin passing them out to the boys. I slunk my shoulders, bowed my head, and made my voice low and respectful.

"These are such beautiful instruments, Padrone. But you were right. I am much too stupid to learn to play a harp or violin. My mama may have said I was a bright boy, but that was just her mother's heart," I said, barely lifting my eyes to his face.

I took a deep breath. "Better I take the triangle so I will not shame you by performing poorly on the street."

He grunted. "Just bring home the money. I don't care what you play."

The little triangle was child-sized, and small enough to fit into a pocket if I had to run. And I planned on running away. I didn't yet know how to do it, or how I could bring honor to Papa and get money for my family.

But somehow, I would have to figure that out.

# CHAPTER 4

*Containing a grave and shocking event
that may disturb some readers*

"New boys! Listen up. You may think you've come to a city so big you can disappear. But you can't run from me," announced Padrone after breakfast that first day, almost as if he could read my mind. "I have spies everywhere; if you try to leave, I'll find you.

"Let me tell you something more. You are better off here than anywhere else," he went on. This was turning into the longest speech I'd ever heard him utter. "Last year, a boy who ran from me ended up in prison. That's what happens to boys like you who cannot speak English and have no family. They get sent to prison."

I wondered how true that was. Luigi certainly believed it, though. He shuddered a little, like he was swallowing a sob. I saw a tear trickle down his cheek.

"Baby," I hissed, loud enough for everyone to hear. Luigi flushed and swayed, looking about to topple over. He was probably still weak from being seasick. Across the way, the would-be thief from last night—I was sure it was him—nodded at me with a sly smile.

I didn't really mean to make Luigi cry harder. The truth is, I felt pretty much the same way. But this was no place to show weakness. By speaking out, I would make my own mark with the other boys.

Besides, I thought Padrone would be pleased if I seemed to be cooperative. I needed to do more to get on his good side. I was sure Signor Ferri warned him that I was a troublemaker and a thief, a boy not to be trusted. And if Padrone watched me like a hawk all the time, my chances of escape would be slim.

I tell you this so you can see just how little I knew.

Because what happened next was this: Before I could move, Padrone grabbed me and threw me to the floor. "Marco and Luigi, sit on his legs. Now!"

At first, the cousins stood still, mouths open in surprise. They inched forward uncertainly. The padrone had made it easy for them, pushing me to the floor. I thrashed and kicked like a pig about to be slaughtered while Luigi and Marco tried to hold me down.

Padrone called for more help. "Giuseppe, these boys are useless. Sit on his legs."

Out of the corner of my eye, I saw the would-be thief from last night come close.

"Stop! Let me go!" I howled.

Padrone gripped my jaw with one large hand, turning my left eye and cheek to the floor. I saw a quick flash of silver—a knife.

Now, here is perhaps more truth than you care to hear: When I saw that sharp, gleaming blade come close to my face, I almost wet my pants. I felt sure he was about to cut my throat or poke out my eye.

I tried to push his arm away, but I was pinned. My heart thumped; the breath flew out of me. His elbow was pressing against my throat. My scream came out a weak, silly screech.

He leaned in closer, pressing hard on my chest. His face was matter-of-fact. He wasn't smiling; he wasn't frowning. The man might have been cutting a piece of bread, not the flesh of a boy. Padrone's sour, stale breath hit me full in the face. Suddenly an image of Old Biter came into my head. I opened my mouth to bite him, which threw him off slightly.

I felt a stabbing, sharp pain. The next instant, I was free. I rolled away, grabbing the right side of my upper lip. I tasted red, salty blood, which began running down my hand in little rivulets. *What just happened?*

"Next," Padrone instructed, his voice flat. Padrone jerked his head at me. "Rocco, bring Luigi here."

I couldn't move. Luigi squealed and pleaded. Giuseppe grabbed him. Luigi lay still and whimpering. Marco was next. They both wet their pants. It was all over in ten minutes.

Then Padrone said, almost pleasantly, as he wiped his

blade on his shirt, "There, all done. You are part of us now."

That's when I finally looked more closely at the faces around me. Each of Padrone's boys—every single one—had a scar on the right side of his upper lip.

While Padrone busied himself with a last-minute repair to a violin, we waited. The boy called Giuseppe sidled up next to me as if we were old friends.

"Don't worry. All the padroni do it," he whispered with a shrug. "Right side, left side, middle—each padrone who keeps street musicians has his own spot."

"But . . . but why?" I said, pressing the back of my hand to my lip.

"To keep track of us. We don't speak English. If one of us tried to run away, of course we'd go to someone from home, someone in Little Italy," he explained. "Everyone in this neighborhood knows the padroni keep street musicians. The mark warns other Italians not to help. It also shows who each boy belongs to, and where he should be returned if he is foolish enough to escape."

I took in this information. "So, no one has ever tried?"

Giuseppe was about to answer when Signor Ancarola hollered, "Silence. I do not need you chattering like birds."

I pressed the end of my shirt to my aching lip, making a dark stain on the cloth. Getting away would be much, much harder than I'd imagined.

Padrone handed out instruments, then passed out thin coats from a pile in the corner. He gave me a triangle with a little stick attached. Luigi and Marco got a harp so tall it towered over them.

"Tonight I will give you lessons. I have no time now," said Padrone. He began to bark out orders. "Spread out. Don't stand on the same street corners. Do not spend the pennies you get. Remember, you must bring a dollar back to me here at Forty-Five Crosby Street. Understood?"

Marco and Luigi sniffled. Tears still ran down their faces. Not me. Giovanni Ancarola wouldn't make me cry. Then a thought popped into my head.

Forgetting Mama's advice to think before speaking, I blurted it out. "How will we know?"

My lip was already swollen and puffy. I felt as if I was talking through thick syrup.

"What do you mean, how will you know?" Padrone snapped.

At first, back in Calvello, I'd thought Signor Ancarola handsome, with his oily black hair and fancy clothes. Now I saw he had no laugh lines around his eyes. He didn't smile enough for that. Perhaps his life was hard too. I suppose it can't have been easy trying to make a living from a bunch of wayward boys. And here I was, buzzing in his ears like a noisy, annoying fly.

I'm not saying I forgive Padrone for that scar on my

lip, a scar I have to this day. But, well, you have to see it from his point of view. He'd gone to a lot of trouble to get us. He was doing what everyone else here did—hustling the best he knew how.

"How will we know how much a dollar is?" I persisted. "Unless you teach us about American coins, we won't know when we've got a dollar."

Padrone was done with me; he was ready to be rid of all of us. "Get your new friend Giuseppe to show you.

"Remember, find your own corner if you have a violin or triangle. The harps need two people to push." Padrone clapped his hands, as if shooing a flock of birds from a field of grain. "Now go! I didn't pay your passage to America so you could sit around and get fat."

I pushed past Marco and Luigi, leaving them to struggle with the large, bulky harp. What they were going to play on it, I couldn't imagine. At least, it was on wheels. By the time I reached the street, I saw that most of the boys had already turned the corner.

I called to Giuseppe, who was trotting away with a violin tucked under his arm. "Hey, what about helping us with the American money?"

"Ah, don't worry. You'll figure it out soon enough," he said with a wave of his hand.

Luigi and Marco were behind me, still struggling to push their battered old harp along the bumpy cobblestones. I thought of the painting in our church in Calvello with two cherubs carrying a harp. It was Mama's favorite. Marco and Luigi were nothing at all like those winged angels—they were pitiful little boys. Somehow, though, looking at them made me pull the piece of bread out of my pocket. I tore it in two, then walked back a few steps and thrust it at them.

"Stop blubbering," I ordered. "It won't help."

"Rocco, wait!" Marco yelled after me as I walked away. "We don't know where to go."

"I don't like it here. I want to go home," Luigi whined.

"Just make sure you memorize this street corner so you can recognize it again," I told them.

That was all the help I gave. I didn't stop. I had other things on my mind. I needed to get away from that rancid, rat-infested den. I had to think. I couldn't worry about anyone else.

My first task, I decided, was to figure out where I was and what New York City was like. Then I could make a plan. I turned a corner and my new world rushed in to meet me.

# CHAPTER 5

*I encounter meddlers
and am tormented by a sausage*

Like a tiny fish swept from a quiet stream into a gushing river, I now found myself on a broad avenue. I remembered this big street from last night. It had been busy then, but nothing like this. Before I could catch my breath, I was carried along by a great wave, a moving, jostling, noisy crowd.

Everyone (except me, of course) seemed to know exactly where to go. Some people were silent, eyes fixed ahead. Others jabbered incessantly. I caught phrases of Italian, as well as other languages I couldn't understand.

I let myself be carried along for a while, the way the ocean currents had carried our ship. It was like nothing I had ever experienced—it was clamor and colors, smells good and bad, movement, energy, a racket of sensations. Then, for the first time since leaving home, I felt something break loose inside, as though I'd been holding my breath for weeks.

I was in America.

I might be no more than a prisoner, and a marked one at that. Yet, for a few bright moments, none of that mattered. I, Rocco Zaccaro, a peasant boy from a far-away hillside, had journeyed across the sea to stride the streets of a great city.

Then something cold and wet brushed my nose like a feather. It happened again. It had begun to snow.


The snowflakes were fluffy, soft things. They were wet and incredibly large. It wasn't long before I could scoop some up and pat them together. I held the cold ball to my stinging lip. It felt good.

I kept walking. Sometimes I left the wide, busy avenue to wander on narrow side streets. Then, before long, I'd find it again. I began to recognize the letters for this street: B-R-O-A-D-W-A-Y. Soon I'd come to know the streets of Lower Manhattan almost as well as the mule paths and twisting alleyways of tiny Calvello. On that first day, all I could do was meander, openmouthed, in a muddled haze.

I crammed my triangle into the pocket of the thin coat Padrone had given me. I knew if I returned empty-handed, he would beat me. I pushed the thought aside the way you kick a pebble out of your path. Later. I would think about that later.

For now, it was still morning and there was so much to take in. Each street corner brought something new. Sharp, delicious smells of baking bread, frying meat and onions, and roasting chestnuts beckoned me around corners and down alleyways. I'd never seen so much food.

The snow didn't let up. I began to shiver. Sometime in the afternoon, I slipped into the covered doorway of a little Italian grocery to shake flakes off my arms and hair. I glanced at my feet. Some of the other boys in the den had been barefoot. When my one pair of shoes wore out or got too small, I might have to go without too.

Suddenly I heard angry shouts in the street. I stuck my head out into the falling flakes to look. The noise was coming from up the way, where some sort of vehicle packed with people—a sort of horse-drawn bus—had stopped.

A man came out of the shop holding a large, juicy sausage wrapped in paper. The smell of it—spicy and hot—made my mouth water. For a second, I thought he might offer me some. Then he opened his mouth and took a gigantic bite.

"Mmm," he murmured in appreciation. I sighed.

I gestured toward the ruckus and asked in Italian, "Can you tell what those people are yelling about?"

"*Sì*, my English is pretty good. Been here ten years; I

even went to the Italian school." He stuck his head out to look, then listened for a moment. He chuckled.

"See that man with the top hat, the one flinging his arms in the air? That's Henry Bergh, and he's making the driver take the horses out of harness. Henry Bergh is called the Great Meddler. Everyone knows him." He took another bite of his sausage and chewed, wiping a thin line of juice from his mouth.

I could hardly stand to watch him eat. I couldn't bear to leave the sausage either. "Why do they know him?"

"Bergh is the animal-rights man." He went back to chewing. "I've seen him out here, rain and shine, making trouble for drivers or investigating ruts in the street and all sorts of foolishness."

"So, what's he doing now with those horses and that . . ." I fumbled for a word, but I'd never seen anything quite like it before. "What kind of vehicle is that, anyway?"

He eyed me closely as he adjusted the paper around the rest of the sausage. Was he suspicious because he could see the fresh blood drying on my lip? "I can see you're a greenhorn. Fresh off the boat, are you?"

I nodded, trying to look as pathetic as I could. Maybe he'd feel sorry enough to give me the rest of his sausage. Or a bite. One bite! I suppose, though, it's easier to feel pity for a boy like me than to actually sacrifice a mouthful of delicious sausage.

"That's a horse-drawn omnibus. It gets people from one part of the city to another," he said finally, without making a move to hand over his sausage. He nibbled some more. It was disappearing fast. "It's like a streetcar."

Noticing my frown, he explained. "Streetcars are pulled by horses too, only they run along a special steel rail in the middle of the road, which makes for a smoother ride. We have both here."

"Why is the man stopping it?"

"Well, if you ask me, Bergh likes to bother folks who're just trying to make a living. Right now he's yelling about how there are too many passengers for the horses to pull in this storm on account of it being too slippery. He's making all the people get off and wants the driver to take the horses back to the stable."

I looked more closely now. The horses stood still, their heads lowered, flanks heaving with hard breaths. I did feel sorry for them. If they worked for Giovanni Ancarola, no one would come to save them.

Then I noticed that Henry Bergh wasn't alone. A small, slight figure stood by the door of the vehicle, gesturing for everyone to get off. I pointed. "Who's that?"

"Ah, everyone knows her too!" He grinned. "That's Meddlin' Mary, Mick Hallanan's daughter. Hallanan is an Irishman who's made good for himself. They call him the Greenwich Village Blacksmith.

"The blacksmith is somehow all tied up with Bergh," the man went on with a shrug. "Can't understand the fuss myself. Horses are just living machines, after all. It's like they say, 'Horses are cheaper than oats.'"

I thought about that. If horses were cheaper than oats, was it the same with boys like me? Were street musicians cheaper than macaroni?

Meddlin' Mary looked about my own age. Her dark hair was pulled into a braid that hung down her back. A bright red scarf was wrapped around her neck. I could hear one of the passengers, a man dressed like a fancy gentleman, yelling at her.

Even so, Mary kept smiling at him. She didn't cower or seem the least bit afraid. I thought of my sister Anna, the only other girl I knew as bold as this. I thought of my promise to her. Yes, Anna would like it here in this noisy, enormous city. Calvello was too small for her.

"Why do they call her Meddlin' Mary?" I asked.

"Because she meddles—interferes." He put his finger on his nose and looked down at me. "Sticks her nose where it doesn't belong. That's what she does—like old man Bergh and other members of his animal-rights society. Hmph!"

He met my eyes then. "I don't meddle, kid. So don't expect help from me."

The sausage was nearly gone.

"I didn't ask for anything!" I protested, unable to take my eyes off it. I knew it was the most delicious sausage in the world. (Well, except for Mama's sausages, of course.)

I realized he wasn't just talking about a sausage. I wouldn't find help here. Now that I was branded one of Signor Ancarola's boys, no immigrant, even someone from my own region of Italy, would dare to give me a hand. The man's next words showed me he'd been thinking along the same lines.

"I don't know exactly what goes on over there on Crosby Street. But let me give you some advice, greenhorn," he went on in a softer voice, as though some part of him did feel sorry for me. "On a day like this, you're better off with a roof over your head than being out alone. It can't be that bad. Just do what your padrone tells you."

"What about another padrone?" I asked. Maybe, I thought, I could work for someone else and still make money to send home.

The man shook his head, touched a hand to his lip, and was silent.

My fingers closed around the cold metal of the triangle in my pocket. This stranger was probably right. Running away today—or maybe any day soon—was foolish. Where would I go? I knew nothing about this strange city. I couldn't just leave without a way to get money. After all, Papa and Mama were depending on that contract. If I left my padrone, they'd get nothing more.

I sighed. Then I did ask him for something. "Can you give me a dollar?"

The man threw back his head and laughed so hard snot ran out his nose. "You're a cocky beggar, ain't you?"

Reaching into his pocket, he handed me a small coin. "Here's a dime. Get nine more of these and you'll have your dollar. If you get a small brownish one, that's a penny. You need a hundred of those to make a dollar. Now get lost. I don't want any trouble with the padroni."

"*Grazie.*" I pocketed the coin. I thought of that sharp silver knife in Padrone's hand. Who could blame this man for wanting to stay clear of trouble?

The man opened his mouth to pop the last bit of sausage in. For a moment, I was so desperate I thought about asking for the paper the meat had been wrapped in, just so I could lick the juice from it. But, heaving a deep sigh, I walked away.

For some reason, I went toward the omnibus. I'd never seen one before. I slogged through the slush, feeling the cold wet creep through my pants where the snow was deepest. The girl called Mary Hallanan was still there, watching each passenger get off. Snowflakes patterned her hair like a piece of lace.

She saw me and smiled. Maybe she thought I'd come to help. There must have been more dried blood on my face than I realized, because when I got close, she raised her hand to her own lip, as if she knew mine must hurt.

It was the first time anyone had given me a friendly smile for a long time. I started to smile back. That made my lip crack open again, and I ended up scowling instead. All at once I felt a burst of anger surge inside. This strong, pretty girl was looking at me with pity— like one of the horses she was trying to save.

I don't really know why I did it. I marched right up to

her and spat near her feet, a big glob tinged with red that spread in the snow. The girl jumped back, startled. She opened her mouth to say something, but I was already stomping off.

I'd only gone a few steps when—*smack!*—something smashed into my back so hard I almost stumbled. I whirled. A mistake. A ball of snow exploded against my chest. Then another.

*"Fermati!"* I yelled. Stop! I began screaming, hurling every insult I knew in Italian.

Not that it would do any good. This Mary girl probably didn't understand Italian any more than I understood English. She patted some snow together, pulled back her arm, and aimed. *Whack!* She got me again.

I sloshed through the mud and slush as fast as I could to the side of the street. Mary wiped her hands together to shake the snow off. She raised her hand at me in a wave and then, suddenly, started to laugh.

I could hardly believe it. So *this* was America. I'd been in my new home less than a day. In that short time, a thief in the night had crept up to take whatever I had, I'd been scarred with a knife, and now I'd been attacked with hard balls of snow by a girl. A girl who then laughed at me!

I heard chuckles erupt all around me. Even the passengers who'd been forced off the omnibus seemed to find the whole incident funny. The man with the sausage hadn't gone back inside. Grinning, he wiped his greasy hands on his pants and called out something to the girl in English.

"What'd you say?" I wanted to know.

"I told her she had good aim," he said. "Now go on back to your padrone. And watch your step in this neighborhood. Pick on the wrong person and next time you could end up with more than a snowball bouncing off your back."

# CHAPTER 6

*I meet the Prince of Bandits' Roost*

I hope all this talk of sausages hasn't made you as hungry as I felt right then. And even though more than anything I longed to bite into something juicy and hot to fill my empty stomach, that didn't happen. All I got that day was more trouble.

I wandered for what seemed like hours, bedraggled and miserable as a chicken in a hailstorm. I even began to worry a little about Marco and Luigi. I couldn't imagine how they'd be able to push that big harp through this slush. Maybe they would look so pathetic people passing by would feel sorry for them and dribble coins into their grubby palms. Yes, perhaps Luigi would end up with two dollars, with enough extra to buy hot chestnuts from a street peddler.

Then I remembered: This was Luigi, after all. Distracted, daydreaming Luigi. It was more likely that he'd forget about the harp completely. Even now he might be sitting in a pile of snow, playing like my little brother, Vito, used to in the autumn leaves back home.

The colder I got, the more I started thinking about the den at 45 Crosby Street. It had a roof. There would be a little food. Oh, I know I talked a big story about making a daring escape from the knife-wielding Giovanni Ancarola. What can I tell you? He might have been a vicious padrone, and the cellar might have been smelly and grimy, but it sure beat freezing on a street corner.

*Just for a few days,* I told myself. *I'll leave once I learn my way around the city and find another way to make money.*

If I wanted to return to Padrone's den that night, I had a problem. Well, two problems. First, I'd have to find Crosby Street again. Second, and more important, I had to get ninety more cents. Otherwise, I could guess what Padrone would do: beat me, or maybe leave me on the doorstep all night. That's what I'd do if I was making the rules.

I straightened my shoulders and took a deep breath. It was time to work. I found a corner where I could stand a bit protected under the overhang of a building. I pulled the little triangle and the stick from my coat pocket and stared at it for a minute. I had no idea how to play it.

Shrugging, I began hitting the thing, making up my own little rhythm. *Ting ting tingaling ting. Ting ting ting tingaling ling.*

The snow had become a light but steady rain. People walked by with heads bent, eyes glued to the ground. Who could blame them? The slush was now almost knee-deep in places. I'd already fallen twice. In the streets, piles of manure mixed with mud and melted snow to make a foul, smelly soup.

I'd put on the socks Anna gave me, but my thin shoes were soaked through. I couldn't feel my toes. My hands were red as tomatoes. I hit my triangle again, louder this time. *Ting ting tingaling TING. Ting ting ting tingaling LING.*

Five minutes. Ten minutes. No one even looked at me. I tried pushing myself into people's faces, using the English words the man with the sausage had taught me. "A dollar. A dime. A penny."

The sky grew darker, the wind whistled fiercely. I got three pennies, then a nickel. I stuck them in the pocket with the one thin dime. Then it happened.

They came around the corner and were on me before I had a chance to cry out. There were three, all taller and broader than me. One grabbed my hands and held them behind my back, sending the triangle and stick spiraling to the ground. The other two were in and out of my pockets so fast I hardly felt my clothes rustle.

*"Grazie,"* a voice hissed in my ear.

One boy pushed my chest with his hand. My feet slipped out from under me and I fell backward. Cold, wet slush seeped through my pants. I bit my bottom lip, but that made my top lip start to bleed again. I could feel the sting of hot tears in my throat. *It's not fair! I shouldn't even be here.*

If only I hadn't shamed Papa. If only I could have told the truth. I swallowed the tears. I wouldn't let myself cry. I would not.

A minute later, a boy stopped in front of me and held out his hand. "Need some help up?"

I dropped my eyes, my breath still coming in gasps. I didn't want more trouble.

"Come on. Up with you, my little friend," he urged. He spoke an Italian that rang familiar in my ears. He might not be from Calvello itself, but he was from somewhere in the south of Italy. Just that was comforting, like hearing the music of the bells of our church back home. "I won't hurt you. Me and Carlo here saw what those street rats did, didn't we?"

"We sure did, Tony." The second boy, shorter and wider than the first, nodded vigorously and grinned. I glanced at him. He was a shadow, a follower. The boy called Tony was in charge.

Without waiting any longer, Tony took hold of my wrist and pulled me up. I leaned over to fish my instrument out of the slush. I felt myself grow red with shame.

"*Grazie,*" I mumbled.

Tony was a head taller than me. I guessed he was fourteen or fifteen, about the same age as the thieves. He leaned over to peer at my face, then grabbed my chin hard and lifted it up to inspect my lip. He was so close I could see that his eyes were almost black.

"Just as I thought—you're a fresh cut," he said. "One of Signor Ancarola's, are you?"

"*Sì,*" I admitted. "This is my first day in the city."

"A real greenhorn! Not having an easy time of it, are you?" He cuffed me lightly on the shoulder, as if we were old friends. "Well, don't worry. Folks here, especially around Mulberry Bend, well, they don't always give newcomers a warm welcome. You'll soon figure out what's what."

I looked at him closely. He sported a warm coat, a vest, and a smart bowler hat. He seemed more like a gentleman than a laborer, which, I knew, most Italian immigrants were. Tony had no scar on his lip, yet clearly he knew the neighborhood. He'd even recognized the way the padroni marked their boys. Whoever Tony was, whatever Tony did, he wasn't under the thumb of a padrone. I could use someone like this on my side. Maybe Tony would be the key to escape, to a job, to money.

"I almost had enough to bring my padrone the dollar I owe him," I lied, shaking off my feelings of weakness. No need for him to know just how poorly I'd been doing.

I rubbed my wrist where one of the other boys had twisted it. "And now I have nothing. You have fine things, and you don't look hungry either. How do you make *your* money?"

Tony flashed a sly smile. "Not so fast there. I don't

make a habit of confiding in greenhorns just off the boat."

"I may be just a greenhorn, but I learn fast," I declared boldly. "I won't be jumped again like that. I have a rule: I only make a mistake once."

Tony stuck his hands in the pockets of his coat, a coat so much thicker than the thin, ratty one I wore. He looked me up and down for a long minute. At last, he grinned. "I think I might like you, kid. You've got a spark, yet you also have a sweet, innocent face. What about you, Carlo? Does this guttersnipe have what it takes?"

Carlo took one step forward and peered at me. He had a crooked nose, which gave his face an odd appearance, as though everything was off balance. I already knew what his answer would be. Carlo would say or do whatever Tony wanted.

"Sweet, but awful skinny, Tony. Might be useful as a stall. Or maybe he's quick enough to dip in and out like a flash," said Carlo. Then he added quickly, "Of course, no one is as fast as you, Tony."

I had no idea what he was talking about, but I smiled as Tony steered me by the elbow into an alley. Several sets of rickety wooden stairs led to the rear doors of tenement houses that loomed on either side. Despite the storm, someone had left clothes hanging on lines overhead. On one side, a plank rested on two barrels, making a kind of bed. The ground was littered with garbage.

Tony and Carlo herded me into a corner, and for an

instant I was afraid the two of them might decide to beat me up just for the fun of it. I certainly had nothing else on me worth stealing.

Instead, Tony laid his arm over my shoulder and grinned, exposing one jagged bottom tooth. "Tell you what, greenhorn. Carlo and me, we admire a kid with spirit. And we think that with a face like yours, you have what we call *potential*.

"So we're prepared to do you a favor," Tony added, giving my shoulder a friendly squeeze. "We'll take you back to Crosby Street and fix it with Signor Ancarola so you won't get in trouble."

I considered. "But . . . why would you do that for me?"

"It's like this. We call this alleyway Bandits' Roost," he said. "I'm the Prince, and this is my base of operations. I say what goes on here. Those alley rats were out of line to take advantage of an innocent like you. I figure it's up to me to make it right."

"How about I stay here? I can work for you right away," I suggested eagerly.

"Hmm, well, I can't take on an unripe fruit like you just yet," he told me. "You need to find your feet, learn your way around. For now, the best I can do is to get you back and make sure you don't get a beating. Right, Carlo?"

"That's right, Tony," said his shadow, nodding fiercely. Carlo's off-balance face made me feel as if I was back on the rolling decks of the *Elysia* again. "That Ancarola is a mean bull. You got to be careful crossing that one."

"Oh, I'm not worried about the padrone," I boasted. "I'm already one of his favorites."

Now, as you well know, that was perhaps stretching the truth just a little. But I desperately wanted to impress this Prince. I could already imagine Papa's neighbors gathering in the piazza to admire me if I returned to Calvello looking as successful as Tony.

*There goes Rocco Zaccaro, who made good in America,* they'd say. *Old man Ferri sent him away in disgrace, but it makes you wonder if there was more to that story.*

I was so caught up in my daydream I jumped a little when Tony patted me on the back. "That's the spirit," he said. "So what do they call you?"

"Rocco. Rocco Zaccaro."

"All right, Rocco, come along with us."


I followed Tony and Carlo through a maze of streets, like a little lamb tripping along blindly behind two shepherds. It was dark when I recognized the cobblestone street and the saloon at 45 Crosby Street.

"It's around back," I said, thinking Tony would come in.

Instead, he stopped, reached into his pocket, and dropped a few coins into my palm. "This is as far as we go. Here's a dollar, with an extra dime to boot. This should help you get on his good side."

"*Grazie.* I'll pay you back someday."

"I'll be sure you do." Tony reached up to adjust the

brim of his smart hat. "That's one of my rules, you see: Anyone who owes the Prince of Bandits' Roost pays his debts."

He grinned like it was a joke. I smiled back. Then, holding tight to my fistful of coins, I set my shoulders and started for the door.

Padrone was in the doorway, shooing another straggler inside and grumbling about the storm. He scowled and gave me a push. "You're the last. I thought you must've got lost, or done something stupid—like try to run away."

The room reeked even worse than it had that morning. The stench of wet coats and shoes, combined with the stale sweat of unwashed bodies, made my stomach lurch. The one coal stove was useless against the dank, chilly air.

I spotted Luigi and Marco slumped in a corner. Luigi tried to smile at me, then stopped and put a hand to his lip. I knew why. All day, every word or movement of my mouth had made my own cut start to bleed again. I gave him a tiny nod, feeling a stab of regret that I'd abandoned them that morning.

Padrone limped to the middle of the room and threw his arms up in dismay. "You boys look to me to feed you all. You complain if your breakfast or dinner is a little short. How am I supposed to pay for food and the roof over your heads when you don't do what you're asked?"

He shook his head. "I'm disgusted. A little snow and you fall to pieces. Not one of you has come back with a whole dollar."

I looked around and let the silence stretch out. Then I stepped forward and held out my hand.

"I have, Padrone," I said. "I earned a dollar—and an extra dime besides."

# CHAPTER 7

So there you have it. That was my first, miserable day as a street musician, struggling to earn a single dollar by striking a little triangle and begging for coins. The best part had been meeting Tony and Carlo. But though I continued to watch for them every day, I never spotted them. They seemed to have been swallowed up by the city, two drops in an ocean of people.

I can't say the same for that girl, the one they called Meddlin' Mary. I encountered her again a few weeks later, after a big April rainstorm had turned the streets into rivers of mud and manure. I came around a corner into a side street and there they were—the girl and that same old man, the Great Meddler—frowning over a deep, uneven hole in the paving stones.

Curious, I stepped behind a telegraph pole to watch. Mary peered up at a street sign, then jotted something in a notebook. Mr. Bergh bent down and unfolded a wooden ruler. He moved around the big rut, placing the ruler here and there, all the while calling out to Mary, who seemed to be recording what he said in a small black notebook.

Suddenly a horse-drawn cab came barreling around the corner. Without missing a beat, Mary waved for it to go around them, her dark braid flying as she flung her arms into the air. Meddlin' Mary could stop traffic!

*What could possibly be so fascinating about a hole in the street?* I wondered. The mystery was solved the next week, when I passed the same place and spied two men at work filling the gap, making the spot with the worn-away, broken stones smooth again.

Horses! That was the answer. Mr. Henry Bergh and Mary Hallanan (and I suppose there were others too) were trying to make the city safer for horses. Somehow, they knew how to get things done, things as small as filling a single gap where a horse might trip.

After that, I began to see Mary everywhere, especially if I wandered west, toward Greenwich Village. Sometimes she carried a book or two, other times that black notebook. Often I would spot her standing on a corner, watching horses as they passed or gazing fixedly down at the mishmash of stones and pavements that made up the city streets. Her movements were so regular I decided she must have had her own route to patrol.

But watching Meddlin' Mary (and, I admit, some-times even looking for her) led to something unex-pected. I began to notice horses too. It just crept up on me, gradual-like, and once I started, I couldn't stop.

I'd pass a gap in the road and wonder if Mary and Mr. Henry Bergh would get it fixed before a horse fell in and broke a leg. I noticed horses so thin their ribs showed. Every week, I saw drivers unhitching fallen horses and leaving carcasses in the gutter. And, of course, omnibuses and streetcars pulled by two horses were everywhere. They were, I realized, always packed to overflowing, making heavy loads for the poor animals.

Then came the day when I saw a driver beating a team struggling to move a heavily loaded wagon. The horses' legs were shaking, their heads bowed. They were doing their best. It made me so mad I began banging my triangle and shouting at the driver in Italian. He shot me an annoyed look and eventually stopped, though he probably didn't understand a word I said.

*It's a good thing Old Biter stayed in Naples with the sailor,* I found myself thinking. *That donkey wouldn't like New York City one bit.*

By now I could play a few different rhythms on my triangle—enough to coax occasional smiles from pass-ersby and entice them to drop a penny or nickel into my palm. Most nights, I made it back by dark with my dol-lar. When I didn't, I curled up against the locked door, often with Luigi and Marco, who couldn't quite get the hang of strumming their big harp. Sometimes Padrone took a paddle to those of us who didn't meet our quota. The less said about that, the better.

Truth was, most of the boys knew only one or two tunes; their violins sounded like screeching cats. There was an exception, though. One spring afternoon, I was searching for a place to play on Elizabeth Street when I saw a small crowd gathered up ahead.

Drawing closer, I caught the sweet, plaintive sounds of a violin. Curious, I pushed to the front. There was Giuseppe, wielding his bow like it was part of his hand. I stayed until the end of the tune, when everyone smiled and applauded and dropped coins into his outstretched hand. Nothing like that had ever happened when I tried to make music.

I asked Giuseppe about it that night.

"I love the violin," he admitted. "But it doesn't do me much good. Padrone knows I can play well. Once he found out that I can easily earn more than a dollar a day, he made me stay in the same spot so he can swoop in to collect anything I've got in my pocket by noon."

That wasn't fair, but by now it didn't surprise me. Giuseppe didn't seem like the sort of boy not to fight back, though.

"You're good enough to be in a real orchestra. Can't you try to hide some money away?" I wanted to know.

"Even if I did, greenhorn, I wouldn't tell you where it was," he said before rolling over on the straw so his back was to me. Giuseppe had his own friends in our den, three boys he had known back home. Marco, Luigi, and I were still newcomers in his eyes and not to be trusted.

Still, despite what Giuseppe said, I didn't feel like a greenhorn anymore. I had picked up a few words of English. I could find my way around Little Italy and recognize street signs. I knew that Crosby was only a block from Broadway, the street that always seemed to me like a great river. Giuseppe told me it led to an enormous space with meadows and trees called Central Park—and even beyond.

"I walked all the way up there once, before Padrone starting watching me so closely," he bragged. "A nice gent had given me a dollar first thing that morning, so I set off to explore. It's like a whole separate city of green, that Central Park. And open to anyone. Even us."

I hadn't managed to go farther north than Fourteenth Street. I kept to the patchwork of streets that made up Little Italy—Broome, Hester, Mulberry, Elizabeth, and Grand—though sometimes I did wander toward the West Village, near Seventh Avenue. (Not that I was trying to catch a glimpse of Meddlin' Mary at work, mind you.) Little Italy was a poor neighborhood. It wasn't always easy to get my daily quota there. But I took comfort in hearing my own language around me.

Despite the run-down tenements, the neighborhood was a humming beehive day and night: workers heading to garment factories, fish and cheese peddlers clustered on a corner, fruit vendors hawking their wares. When people stopped to chat near me, I would catch snatches of conversations, enough to piece together their stories. I heard a man tell another that he'd just earned enough to send for his wife. Friends and relatives seemed to look out for one another.

*It's like Calvello, only bigger. Much bigger,* I realized.

Sometimes I wondered what would happen if I could bring my family here. Papa was used to hard physical labor, so he might work unloading ships at the dock. I could imagine Anna and, when she was older, Emilia striding off to a garment factory with other girls. Mama, who was always thrifty and shrewd, might take in boarders and entice them to stay with her delicious meals. Maybe, with everyone else working, Vito could stay in school.

This was foolish thinking, I knew. Mostly, I stood in the midst of noisy, chattering crowds, feeling so alone I began to talk to my little triangle. "How are you doing today?" I'd whisper. "Will you ring brightly for me so we can earn our dollar quickly?"

I know you're probably laughing at me now. Snicker if you must. All I can say is that my loneliness felt as real as pain. Sometimes sharp, like a knife cut; other times dull, like the endless ache of hunger.

And while most days I wanted to be like Tony, who strutted like a prince, there were moments when I thought I'd be happy to do real work, just as I'd done back home. Every day in New York, I saw boys sweeping sidewalks and shops, selling newspapers, and hurrying here and there carrying messages of all sorts.

But this? Anything would be better than being kept in a den. Anything would be better than being a beggar.

# CHAPTER 8

*In which I receive an intriguing invitation*

"So, here you are," crooned a voice in my ear one afternoon in early summer.

I whirled, ready to pounce or run to protect my earnings. It hadn't been a bad day so far. The warm breeze and sunshine seemed to lift people's spirits, and I already had fifty cents.

"Tony!"

"That's right, your first friend in the city. Let's take a look at you." Tony stood back, folded his arms across his chest, and gazed at me solemnly.

He shook his head and sighed. "What do you think, Carlo? Rocco's been here quite a few weeks now, but he looks as much like a bedraggled alley rat as he did the first day."

Almost without thinking, I touched my tongue to the scar on my lip. It was still there, it would always be there—a reminder of what I now was. Padrone's boys went to the public baths once a month, and wore their clothes until they fell off. My shirt was caked with dried mud; both sleeves were ripped. My pants reached only to the top of my ankles. Somehow, even with little food, I'd grown an inch since March.

I was definitely a pathetic-looking creature. For his part, Tony glowed with good health, as smart and sleek as a spirited young colt. He sported a nifty vest and a stylish bowler hat. And his shoes! Oh, they were beauties, made of real brown leather. Even on these dusty streets, they shone. They were exactly the sort I dreamed of wearing one day, the kind of shoes to make Papa proud of me again.

At Tony's shoulder, Carlo grinned. "I hate to say it, Tony, but Rocco still looks like a greenhorn to me."

"I am not!" I protested, jutting out my chin. "I can find my way around just fine, and I haven't been robbed once since that first day." That, at least, was true.

"Good for you," Tony said wryly. "And how are you getting along as a street musician?"

"I do all right," I told them. I couldn't resist lying, just a little. "I haven't been short my dollar quota even once."

"Yet you haven't tried to escape," Tony pointed out.

"No," I admitted. "But I will. Soon."

That, as I was sure Tony realized, was another lie. It was perfectly plain I was nothing more than a fly stuck in my padrone's web.

Why hadn't I tried? I could pile up excuses one by one until they were as tall as a great building: I'd been sick, coughing through much of the spring; I didn't want to starve; I was still trying to figure out a plan so I wouldn't get caught; I worried about my parents losing the money Padrone had promised them each year.

The truth was, I was in a muddle. I didn't know where to begin. I couldn't imagine how to change my life.

Tony made a tsk-tsk sound with his tongue. "I'm disappointed, Rocco. I expected a sharp lad like you to be free of your padrone by now—or at least have the gumption to try."

Then, leaning close, he whispered conspiratorially, "Maybe we can help you out again."

He grinned, exposing his jagged tooth. If Tony ever had occasion to bite someone, that tooth would definitely come in handy.

That tooth made me think of Old Biter, traipsing happily through the streets of Naples. I wondered if he'd given up his bad habits and now greeted people with a toothy donkey grin. *I bet Old Biter's new owner is just like Meddlin' Mary, making sure he doesn't step in any treacherous holes,* I thought.

"Why would you help me again?" I asked warily.

I felt an odd chill, as if an invisible fog had touched

the air between us. It struck me that this might not be an entirely friendly encounter. I still owed Tony a dollar—a dollar and ten cents, to be exact. It had been so long since I'd seen him I'd almost forgotten about my debt. He, I suspected, had not.

And I *did* owe Tony. Being the only boy to return with a dollar on that stormy March night had raised my standing with my padrone. Signor Ancarola didn't seem to consider me a troublemaker now.

Tony and Carlo led me to an alleyway. It looked familiar. This, I realized, was Bandits' Roost, where we'd come that first day.

"I thought you were different, Rocco—that maybe you'd fight harder than most of those sheep in Padrone's den," Tony was saying. "I thought I saw a spark in you."

Carlo spoke up. "You should've found Tony to pay him back by now. That would have been the way to show thanks and respect. You could've come to Bandits' Roost to find him. Instead, we had to track you down. That's not so good, Rocco."

Carlo shook his head, putting a sad expression on his face. I felt sure they were about to beat me up. Should I try to break free and make a run for it? I didn't see how—my back was to the wall. The two older boys blocked my way.

"I'm sorry," I mumbled. My excuses sounded lame even as I stammered on. "I—I should've tried to f-find you. I—I was so turned around that first day I didn't know where I was. You can have all I have in my pocket. I'll get you the rest tomorrow."

"It's been months since I *loaned* you that money," Tony pointed out. "With interest, the debt is about three dollars now."

"Three dollars!" I protested. "I can't get three dollars right away."

"Temper, temper," warned Tony. He grinned and spoke softly, bringing his face close so that his dark eyes held mine. "Don't be mad. I'm just teasing you a little. You once said you might like to work for me. As it happens, we could use someone like you right now.

"It'll just be a side job, at least at first," Tony went on. "You'll still stay with your padrone until we see how you do. But you can spend part of the day with us and work off your debt. If you apply yourself to the business, well, maybe you'll be able to free yourself from his snare before you know it."

"What kind of job is it?"

"It's best if we show you," said Tony.

"It's a lot more fun than banging a triangle on the street," Carlo assured me cheerily. "And Tony thinks you'll be good at it."

"You have the right sort of face," Tony agreed. "So, Rocco, do you want to make a future for yourself, or stay an alley rat your whole life?"

I took a deep breath. "*Sì*. All right, I'll do it."

What did I have to lose? Besides, I couldn't think how else I'd ever pay Tony back.

"Good. We'll meet you on the corner of Grand and Broadway—not far from Crosby," Tony said. "Be there around eight tomorrow morning."

"I have one more question. If . . . if I work for you part of the day, will I still be able to give my daily quota to Padrone?" I didn't want to get punished any more than necessary.

"Don't worry about that. I guarantee that you'll head home tomorrow night with a dollar," Tony said smoothly. "Just be at the meeting place, and don't let Signor Ancarola or any of the other boys see you. That's important. Can you do that?"

I nodded. And then they were gone.

# CHAPTER 9

Next morning, I stuffed my triangle into my pocket and slipped off, careful to thread my way along side streets to get out of sight as quickly as I could.

The hardest boy to shake was Luigi, who always wanted me to walk with Marco and him. "Please, Rocco," he begged. "Just help us get the harp to Mulberry Street. Marco coughs so much we have to stop all the time so he can rest."

"I can't this morning, Luigi," I told him. Seeing the look on his face, I added, "I'll try to find you at the end of the day and help you get it back here."

He nodded and sighed. He didn't really believe I'd keep that promise. I rarely did. Luigi was so easily distracted and Marco so sick that the two had a hard time making their quota. I'd spotted them just the week before. Luigi had stopped to watch a bunch of boys playing ball in an alley. Marco was leaning against a building with his eyes closed.

Luigi and Marco would just hold me back. I had other plans.

At the corner, I waited nervously. What if they didn't appear? But Tony arrived minutes later, with Carlo right behind him, a burlap bag slung over his shoulder.

"Got the newspapers," Carlo announced.

"Good. Let's go," Tony replied. "We'll walk down Broadway to Wall Street. We want to be near the banks when they open."

"Banks are good," echoed Carlo.

"Why's that?" I asked.

"Lots of potential customers, so to speak," Tony said as he made his way through the throng.

I struggled to keep up, stepping around an elderly man pushing his way down the sidewalk with his cane. "So, you're in the newspaper business?"

"Something like that," replied Tony, adjusting a light coat he'd draped over his arm. The weather was warm, and I wondered why he needed it.

"Will I learn to sell papers too?"

"Hmm ... we'll see," he mused. "Don't worry about that just now. There's a lot to learn first."

"Will you teach me the English words, though?"

Most of the boys at 45 Crosby Street—and even the padroni themselves—didn't know much English. Somehow, they got by, probably because they rarely left Little Italy. Yet, since that first day, when I couldn't understand or yell back at Meddlin' Mary, I'd wanted to learn as much of the language as I could.

"*Sì,* that part is easy," Carlo said, slowing to walk next to me. "First, you hold up a newspaper close to a man's face—right where he can see it. You want the headline to catch his eye. You wave it around."

He pulled one of the newspapers out of his bag to demonstrate. "Then, in English, you say, 'News, boss? Need the news today?'"

"News, boss? Need the news today?" I repeated the phrases until I could say them perfectly. This was already my best day in New York. I was learning to speak English, like a real American.

I'd never ventured as far south as Wall Street on my own before. Tony told me it was close to the tip of Manhattan. "You arrived at Castle Garden, just like we did. It isn't far from where we are now."

This neighborhood seemed like a different city altogether. I was used to dismal, crowded streets lined with tenements, but here we walked by solid stone buildings, some with huge round columns, fancy arched windows, and ornate decorations. The streets weren't packed with vendors and peddlers either. Instead, businessmen hurried by and messengers carrying packets scurried past us, looking busy and important.

As I heard people talking, I could tell that most of these men weren't new immigrants from Italy, Russia, or Poland. Many must be American businessmen. Suddenly I was self-conscious about the way I looked—and smelled. I didn't belong here.

Just as I was feeling like turning around, Tony steered me to a little corner under an overhang of a building. From this spot, I could see the grand double doors of a large building with six or seven wide stone steps leading up to it. Carlo handed me the newspaper he'd been carrying and pulled another from his bag.

"Now, Rocco, all you need to do is stay in this spot. Don't move, and whatever you do, don't talk to anyone," Tony instructed. "If anyone so much as looks at you, just hold up this paper and pretend to be reading. And make sure you hold it right side up. Got that?"

I nodded and held up the paper correctly to show him I knew how. "Do you want me to try to sell a newspaper too?"

"No. Just stand here," Tony repeated. He took a large envelope from the pocket of his coat, then draped the coat over his arm again. "Keep your eyes open—and remember, not a sound out of you. I'm headed for that big bank across the street. Watch me."

With his bowler hat, shiny shoes, and smart clothes, Tony fit right in with the young messengers dashing by. Whistling merrily, and stepping nimbly aside to avoid a horse-drawn cab, he crossed the street to the bank and bounded up the stone steps two at a time.

I turned to say something to Carlo, but he'd disappeared. I held the newspaper in front of my face, leaned against the building, and pretended to read. At first, nothing happened.

A little while later, though, as I peeked over the top of the paper, I caught sight of Tony again. He was coming out of the bank behind a well-dressed older man with a round pink face. On the top step, Tony paused. He coughed and grabbed his right side, as though he had a pain there.

The pink-faced gentleman shuffled slowly down the steps and crossed to my side of the street. When he was almost directly in front of me, Carlo suddenly reappeared, coming up the sidewalk on my right. Carlo was walking so fast he bumped into the man.

"Sorry, boss!" Carlo cried, stopping to steady the man. Then he flashed a newspaper in front of the man's face. "Need the news today?"

As to what happened next, well, I admit I was as bowled over as the sucker himself! All at once Tony was back. He gave no sign that he recognized us. Instead, Tony just strolled by, coming close to the man, pausing for only a second.

The pink-faced gentleman reached into one pocket, then another, to find a coin to pay for the newspaper. His pockets were empty.

"Hey!" the man yelled. "What . . ." He whirled, trying to see who had robbed him.

But he stood alone.

Carlo and the newspaper had disappeared. Tony was gone too, melting into the crowd, but not before he'd slipped his hand into the man's pocket, gently sliding the wallet up and out of it and into his own.

After fuming for a while, the man stormed off, grumbling, "Dratted street bandits."

I did feel a teeny bit sorry for the gentleman. After all, he'd just been minding his own business. However, at that moment, my stomach growled, and I thought of the meager breakfast I'd had. Let's just say my twinge of conscience didn't last very long.

Since coming to America, I'd been hungry every day. Each time I passed someone selling roasted chestnuts, my mouth watered. It was as if breathing in the aroma took me right back to those crisp fall days of gathering nuts in the woods back home.

I will tell you that sometimes on Mulberry Street I'd stolen apples and even potatoes from vegetable carts. Hunger had driven me to do it—and I wasn't the only one. It seemed that every street kid on the Lower East Side did the same. But I'd never imagined doing anything as bold as this.

For, as I am sure you've already guessed, I'd finally discovered the secret to Tony's fine clothes. Tony and Carlo were pickpockets.

# CHAPTER 10

*Of several new matters not expected,*
*including sausages*

I waited. Ten minutes. Fifteen. I began to wonder if Tony and Carlo were coming back for me. Carlo appeared first. Beckoning with a nod, he led me along winding, narrow streets to a little café. Tony was already there.

"I ordered us coffee, sausages, potatoes, and eggs," Tony announced as we slipped into chairs around the small table.

"Sausages?" I gasped. "Did you say sausages?"

And then it happened—three plates were placed before us, one right under my nose. Right under it!

"For me?" I squeaked.

I leaned over to breathe in all the fried, spicy warmth of it. I was almost too excited to eat. Sausages!

"Go ahead, Rocco. Dig in." Carlo grinned and speared a piece of potato, shiny with grease. "You're the best wire in the business, Tony. That touch was as smooth as silk."

I was hardly listening. All I could do was shovel forkfuls of food into my mouth. I noticed Tony staring at me, and realized I was inhaling potatoes faster than a city sewer gulps garbage in a rainstorm. I couldn't seem to slow down.

Then, with a flick of the wrist, Tony performed an act of kindness I'll never forget. A few minutes later, a second plate, steaming and piled just as high as the first, appeared before me. I raised my eyebrows quizzically, wiping the dripping egg from my chin with one hand.

"Just eat it, kid. You look like you need it."

Whatever else you can say about Tony, he still had a heart.

When we'd cleaned every bit of egg and potato grease off our plates with bread, Tony leaned back, cradling his coffee cup in his hands. Carlo sat up straighter. I did too. The mood had shifted, and we were about to talk business.

"Now for the plunder." Tony reached into his pocket and began counting out dollar bills on the table: "One, two, three, four, five, six."

He picked up a dollar and placed it near the edge of the table. "Fifty-five cents for our breakfast, a bit more than usual today, thanks to an extra ten cents to satisfy Rocco's appetite." Tony winked. "I'll keep the change from that dollar, if you don't mind."

"*Grazie.*" I flushed, embarrassed at how fast I'd gobbled down the food. I looked at my plate hopefully. No, it was perfectly clean, not a smudge of grease left.

Tony put another dollar in front of me. "That's your quota for your padrone for the day."

"But . . . but I didn't earn it. And what about the other three dollars I owe you?"

"Well, now you owe me four."

Then he made two piles, one with three dollars, and one with a single bill. "And that's the rest of the plunder, divided between Carlo and me, on account of we were the ones that did the graft."

Carlo scooped up his dollar quick as a frog snatching a fly with its sticky tongue. Tony pulled the last three dollars toward him. "The dip always gets the most, since he takes the most risk."

I stared at the money. All this—in less than five minutes!

"Come to work for me, Rocco, and you'll eat sausages at noon and still be able to pay your padrone," Tony proposed. "No more standing for hours, begging on the corners for pennies."

"Why choose me? There must be hundreds of other boys who'd want to work for you."

"Well, like we said, we think you have the look a real grafter needs—and that's not easy to find," Tony replied.

"You're also quick, and you don't seem afraid of much. Even on that first day, you showed spirit."

He leaned forward, though Tony, unlike Carlo, would never put his elbows on the table. "I'd like to give you the chance to pay me back by working for me. Besides, Carlo and I recently lost the other member of our mob. He took a fall."

"He fell down?" I asked, confused.

My question set Carlo to giggling. He whispered, "Taking a fall means getting arrested."

"A quick little lad like you doesn't need to concern yourself with things like that," Tony assured me. "We'll start you off on a trial basis. You'll learn to be a stall. But you are sworn to secrecy or else . . ."

He let the end of the sentence trail off.

"Rocco, don't pass up this chance. You're perfect for this line of work, with your smooth cheeks and big eyes," Tony went on. "As soon as I saw you standing on the corner in the snow that day, I thought, *This boy has the potential to make lots of money. He has the sweet, innocent face of an angel.*"

*Lots of money!* Tony said I had the chance to make lots of money. Here was the answer to all my problems. And maybe he was right about my face—Mama had called me her angel boy.

"What exactly would I do as . . . um . . . as a stall?"

"The job of a stall is to distract the sucker—the person being robbed," Carlo explained. "I usually act as the stall since I'm not as fast a pick as Tony. I have big, clumsy feet."

He pulled a toothpick from his pocket and began cleaning his teeth. He seemed to have fun no matter what he did. Now he grinned, showing bits of sausage dotting the crevices between his teeth like dark sheep on a bright hillside.

"What I'm good at is talking loud and shoving—creating a distraction," Carlo boasted. "But even with me in the mob, it's definitely safer to use two stalls when you make a touch. That's what Tony says. Right, Tony?"

"That's right." Tony sipped his coffee. "Like today, usually we'd have another stall as backup to Carlo while the pick makes the actual touch. Were you able to follow what we were doing?"

"I think so," I said slowly. "You worked together to position the man to make picking his pocket easy. But how . . . how did you know where the man's wallet was?"

Tony produced the envelope I'd seen earlier. "As I was standing in the bank lobby, supposedly busy checking the contents of this packet, I was actually scouting around for a likely sucker.

"Once I spotted that man with the pink face, all I had to do was watch where he put his leather," he went on. "I signaled that information to Carlo from the steps by coughing and holding my right side. That's how Carlo knew to create a distraction on the sucker's *left* side."

"Leather," I figured, meant wallet. He'd said the word "sucker" in English, so I asked about that.

"The sucker is the target of our operation, Rocco," Carlo told me. "And there ain't anyone more skilled than Tony at spotting them. You're in good hands."

I leaned my elbows on the table and matched Carlo's whisper. "Let me be sure I understand. Carlo, when you waved the newspaper in his face, you were forcing the man to turn toward you so Tony would be free to dip into his other pocket."

"Exactly! I knew you'd be a quick one." Carlo beamed at me and nodded, like a young uncle watching a favorite nephew take his first steps.

"If we have two stalls, I might sometimes pass the plunder to one of you," Tony went on. "That way, if I'm seen with my hand in a pocket and a copper shows up, I'm clean."

He paused. I knew what the next question would be. "So, Rocco, are you in? Do you have what it takes to be a pickpocket?"

Looking Tony straight in the eyes, I nodded. "Actually, I was a pickpocket before. Back home in Calvello."

"You were?" asked Carlo, gazing at me with new respect.

"Yes. I once picked the pocket of Signor Ferri, the richest man in town," I boasted.

But even that was a lie.

# CHAPTER 11

*I embark on a rewarding new pastime,*
*which virtuous readers will undoubtedly*
*find objectionable*

The summer I became part of Tony's mob was by far the most thrilling (and rewarding) chapter in my short life. By the time my twelfth birthday—and the feast of Saint Rocco—rolled around in the middle of August, I'd picked up the tools of my new trade and even added some suggestions of my own.

In other words, I took to grafting like a fish to water. I will admit that from time to time doubts did crop up, like little mushrooms dotting the forest floor after a rainstorm. *What would Mama say if she saw me? Is this really the way to make Papa proud?*

Let's just say that whenever that happened, my stomach stepped in and swept those niggling misgivings away as quickly as my sisters and I could clear a mushroom patch and run home with baskets full of tasty delicacies.

Besides, as I asked myself each night when I lay itching and miserable on the straw of my padrone's den, what other choice did I have? How else could I get out of there?


Tony, Carlo, and I became a smooth-working mob, as finely tuned as a team of high-stepping carriage horses. We perfected our technique all over the area around lower Broadway, from Fulton down to Wall Street. Sometimes we targeted businessmen coming out of a bank after withdrawing money, the way Tony and Carlo had demonstrated. Other times we didn't bother with anything so elaborate.

We got adept at spotting messengers and junior clerks, looking puffed up and important as they made their way to the bank carrying leathers stuffed with dollars. A nod from Tony, and we'd make the touch on a crowded sidewalk, right on the spur of the moment. Older gents remained our favorite targets for two reasons: They usually provided the most plunder, and they didn't move very fast.

It worked like this: I'd stop a fellow and wave a newspaper in his face. Then I'd smile sweetly and say the words Carlo had taught me: "News, boss?"

Before the man could answer, Carlo would come barreling down the sidewalk, just as he had that first morning. Now, though, he'd crash right into me so hard I'd go flying against the sucker.

Carlo would pretend to be angry, yelling that the collision was *my* fault. "Hey, watch where you're going, you little alley rat!"

Carlo was heavier than I was, and his crooked nose (it had been broken, he said, in a fight two years before, when he was twelve) gave him an odd, fierce expression when he set his face into a glare. As he glowered, I would cower and wail for the stranger to protect me.

Once in a while, a man might push me away in disgust. Usually, though, the sucker would reach out to help me, a poor, innocent boy being picked on by a bully. It didn't matter. The end result was the same. While the target focused on me, Tony would be in and out of his pocket in a flash.

Now, while this scheme did require us knowing where the plunder was, I soon found it didn't take more than a few minutes to see where a target was carrying the goods. Nine times out of ten, if the man was right-handed, it would be in his right pocket.

There were other clues too. If a young clerk was carrying a good amount of money, or a messenger was worried about losing his packet to a thief, he'd almost always reach into the pocket we wanted as he walked along, just to reassure himself the bills were still safe. Once our little mob saw him do this, the chance of that money reaching its destination was slim, very slim indeed.

Of course, it's always nice to have variations in routine.

Sometimes Carlo would trip me, and I'd land right on the victim's shoes. The sucker would bend down to help me up (since he couldn't very well walk over me), leaving a pocket exposed and ripe for the picking.

Once we got started, there seemed to be no stopping us. From some fellow grafters, Tony had learned how to "bang a super," or, as we sometimes called it, "get a man's front"—take his watch by detaching it from the chain. This involved some clever handiwork, as Tony had to quickly use his thumb and forefinger to break one of the rings of the chain, then slip the watch free and into his pocket.

To do this, usually Carlo elbowed me in the head as he bumped into the victim and me both. (Come to think of it, I was always the one getting injured.) I'd throw back my head, cover my eye with my hands, and pretend to be even more hurt than I was. (And, believe me, Carlo could be rough.) I'd start wailing in English, "Ow! Ouch! My eye. Sir, will you look at my eye?"

As the gent reached out to take my hands away and examine my eye, Tony would be behind him, deftly reaching around his middle, and have the watch in his hand in a quick minute. At the same time, I'd yelp again, or bark a harsh cough, to mask the sound of the ring breaking, just in case the man happened to hear it.

If the sucker felt a slight brush against his waist, why, he just assumed it was the little monkey squirming in pain in front of him. Once the "super," or watch, was in his hand, Tony would swiftly pass it to Carlo, who would clear out. That way, if the victim got wise and tried to stop Tony, or point him out to a copper, Tony would be clean. By the time the gent noticed his chain dangling, the watch long gone, we'd be gone too.

If I do say so, it went like clockwork every time.

Now, you may well decide that my new pursuits show that Papa was, in fact, quite right to get rid of an incorrigible young scoundrel like me. Yet, as I have remarked previously in this history, that's where the truth of things gets a bit hard to hold on to, at least for me.

Should I have bowed to my padrone's orders day after day without doing anything to try to change my fate? Should I have let myself be worked to death like the cart horses I saw almost every day on the streets?

I don't really know. But I will tell you that there was definitely one benefit of my dangerous new pursuits: I was eating more sausages.

I stayed with Tony and Carlo only through the morning or early afternoon, and was always careful not to be spotted by Signor Ancarola or the other padroni. Since our mob mostly worked in the financial district down by Wall Street, where my padrone wasn't likely to go, I didn't worry about that so much.

The highlight of the day would come around noon, after we'd made our last touch. That's when we went for a meal.

"Don't you ever want to try anything besides sausages?" Carlo asked one day.

Chewing, I shook my head. *Why would I do something like that?*

As I said, the meal was the highlight of the day. When we were done, I'd leave Tony and Carlo and find a likely corner near Mulberry Street, where I'd spend the rest of the afternoon and evening banging on my triangle, or wandering around looking at things.

Once, my padrone came upon me unexpectedly, grabbing my shoulder and growling, "I walked by here an hour ago. Where were you?"

I wasn't frightened. I had seventy-five cents in coins jingling in my pocket to show my progress for the day. Hidden in my shoe was another dollar—insurance. Sometimes Padrone searched our pockets at night to make sure we weren't holding back coins.

But since half the boys didn't even have shoes, he'd never gotten into the habit of checking our feet. So sometimes I'd hide a few coins or even a dollar in my shoe for a rainy day, or in case I wanted to take time off from hitting my triangle to go down to the docks and see the ships—or just wander around looking at the food carts. (Or, I admit, wandering off near Greenwich Village, where I might catch sight of Mary at her work.)

Every day, I'd tell myself I *should* begin saving anything

I didn't hand over to Padrone. I would hold a coin in my hand and resolve to start right away. But it was hard to get started with just one quarter, or dime, or even a dollar. Every once in a while—not often—I'd buy a roll and break it in two for Marco and Luigi to gnaw on at night. Usually, though, I'd walk by a shop and catch the scent of fresh bread or hot, spicy sausages, and my stomach would win out over my head.

One bright summer day, after I'd told Tony I'd never seen this Central Park that Giuseppe had told me about, we even rode a horse-drawn streetcar (which we called a rattler) uptown to a huge green place. We crossed a stone bridge, threw pebbles into a lake, and lay on soft grass that tickled our ears. Best of all, we bought ice cream, so cold and sweet I had to buy two. Naturally, on the rattler on the way there, we made a touch to pay for our food.

There was so much food, everywhere I turned. It wasn't easy to save in a place like New York, where you could get sausages, ice cream, apples, rolls, and sweets of all kinds if you just had the money to buy it.

Money. It was clear I needed more of it.

Then, right around my birthday in August, I came up with a brilliant new strategy: a way to get more money so that I could escape from the padroni den *and* still keep my stomach full.

# CHAPTER 12

*In which I make an audacious proposal*
*of dubious merit*

It all began one day when Carlo mentioned that moll-buzzers were pickpockets who only steal from *women.*

"Moll-buzzers usually have sweet faces," he remarked. "That way, women don't get suspicious when they come close."

My mind began to race with possibilities. I asked, "Have you ever tried it, Tony?"

We were chomping down a midday dinner at Barnabo's Restaurant on Pearl Street. I had my favorite: sausages, of course. Tony was eating chops, and Carlo was devouring pork and beans.

"Naw. Neither Carlo or me has quite the right look," Tony replied. "Carlo's nose is as crooked as Mulberry

Bend, and I'm too tall. You need a sweet, young face to be a good moll-buzzer."

"I have a sweet face," I declared. "You said so yourself the first day we met."

Carlo pointed his fork in my direction. "That's true, Tony. Just look at those soft cheeks and that pert little nose. It's a sight nicer than mine."

"Just this morning, a rich old lady smiled at me," I lied, leaning forward eagerly. "I'd be good at this. Give me a chance, Tony. Moll-buzzing could become my . . . um . . . specialty. It could help us expand into new areas of graft."

Then I added, trying to sound as casual as I could, "And I could be the dip."

Now, I'd been longing to spread my wings, to be the one to hold a gold watch in my hands, but Tony had always said no. If we took up moll-buzzing, something only I was well suited for, then I'd *have* to be the one picking the pockets.

The dip. That was my goal—what I really wanted. The moll-buzzing was just a way to make it happen. I knew Tony would never give me a chance otherwise. He liked getting most of the plunder.

If I could be the dip, I could actually begin to save a lot of money—enough to escape from Padrone before my four-year contract was up and return home to my family in triumph.

This was my new plan—the answer to everything. I just knew it.

I waited. It seemed a long time before Tony answered. He stared out the window, called for a refill of coffee, twirled his spoon on the table. It was as if he was searching for a reason to turn me down. He found one.

"I hate to disappoint you, Rocco," he said finally, frowning slightly. "You may look sweet, but you sure don't smell sweet. You, my little friend, have guttersnipe written all over you."

He shook his head. "You do all right as a stall because it's a matter of seconds, you bumping into a sucker. Hardly long enough for them to get a whiff of you.

"With a woman, it's different," he declared. "You try to get close to a moll, and she's going to back off like she's smelled a skunk."

My heart sank. My plan seemed to evaporate like rain on hot pavement. While I couldn't be sure if Tony was just trying to hold me back, determined to keep the lion's share of plunder for himself, I had to admit there was some truth to what he said.

I stared down at my filthy, torn pants and my grubby shirt with holes in it. My left big toe stuck out of my shoe and was black with dirt. My skin was patterned with bites and sores and covered in a layer of sweat and grime.

"To be a good grafter, you have to do more than look the part," Tony went on, warming to the subject. "You have to *be* the part.

"Take me. I have ambition. I want to be a man of the world—visit the best dance halls, be seen at swell hotels and theaters, spend the day at the horse races. There's real money to be made in those places, but you've got to fit in. You've got to belong."

"What can I do?" I asked. "I can't get new clothes or look clean. If I took a bath even once a week, Padrone would be suspicious. We only get one bath a month. He'd be onto my secret in a second."

"So long as you're a street musician marked by your padrone, there's not much more you *can* do," Tony concluded with a shrug. "You're learning to be a good stall. Stay with it; you might have a future when the contract with your padrone is up."

"That's almost four years from now!"

"Maybe you can escape before then," Tony suggested. "You could save enough to take the train out of here and make a new start somewhere else. I hear Boston and Philadelphia are good cities for grafting."

"Boston or Philadelphia?" I had no idea where those places were, or how I could get there. "Were you . . . are you thinking of moving there?"

"Me?" Tony laughed. "Naw, I'm right where I want to be. Oh, I might on occasion take a train ride to dip into the pleasures of grafting in a new pasture. But New York City is where I belong."

I stared down at my empty plate. "So, no moll-buzzing? No way that I can be a dip?"

"No," said Tony firmly. "Take it from an expert, Rocco. Being a dip is too risky for a smelly street bandit like you."

# BOOK TWO

*Fall 1887*

# CHAPTER 13

*A little chapter*
*containing a small but significant incident*

I can almost hear what you're thinking: *Don't be daft, Rocco, follow Tony's advice!*

I gave myself much the same talking-to over the next few weeks. Alas, by the time the intolerable summer stickiness had mellowed into the soft breezes of September, I'd made up my mind to completely ignore every single thing Tony had told me.

Despite his warnings, I would use my sweet, innocent face to become a moll-buzzer, with the goal of keeping for myself every penny I earned.

Once I'd made my decision, it took me a couple of weeks to get up the courage to put my plan into action. Then, one afternoon after I'd left Tony and Carlo and was heading back toward Crosby Street, I spotted a leather peeking up out of an old woman's pocket. She was ambling along with a slow, steady motion, rocking to and fro like a boat.

*This is it. This is my chance,* I thought.

I bumped her gently, deftly reached into her pocket, slid out the purse, and was gone before she'd even caught her balance.

My heart began to race as I tucked the prize under my shirt. If anyone caught sight of it, that could mean trouble. Tony had told stories of angry passersby descending on a pickpocket like a swarm of infuriated insects, holding him down until a copper showed up to haul him off to jail.

Breathing hard, I managed to slip into a narrow alley near Hester and Mulberry. To my relief, no one was around. I was safe, at least for the moment. I stooped behind some old bins, out of sight in case anyone came. I opened the purse, hoping for riches. Instead, I found four dollar bills.

Four dollars. Not a bad start, but not as good as most touches on Wall Street. I'd already figured that to book passage home to Italy—and bring my parents the sum the padrone would've paid them each year for my services—I'd need more than a hundred dollars. At this rate, it would take months. Still, I had to begin somewhere.

Searching for something I could use as a hiding place, I spotted a loose brick in the ground. I grabbed a sharp-edged broken stone and poked at the brick till I got it free. Then I used the stone to dig a small hole underneath and tucked the money inside.

I fitted the brick back and surveyed my handiwork proudly. Here was the beginning of my secret stash. Like I said, I'd always ended up using any money I'd hidden in my shoe to buy food or pay my padrone. But now I was determined to save these dollars—and begin turning my dreams of escape into a real plan.

So, even though I was now a full-fledged, double-crossing rat who'd gone behind Tony's back to strike out on my own, I just about skipped out of that alley. For the first time in months, I felt hope. I was on my way.

# CHAPTER 14

*Containing some surprising revelations
and a terrible but predictable episode*

One morning not long after the aforementioned incident, Carlo arrived at our meeting place alone to say
he'd stopped to get Tony at his boardinghouse, only to
find him hacking and wheezing.

"Sorry to deprive you of your sausages, Rocco, but
Tony says we should take the day off," Carlo told me.

"Doesn't he think we can do it without him?" I asked,
feeling quite confident after my own recent exploit.
"You're just as experienced as he is, aren't you? Don't
you want to at least give it a try?"

Carlo peered at me, eyes wide, as though it had never
occurred to him to question Tony's instructions. Then
he laughed. "Why not? What have we got to lose? I've
always wanted a chance to be a dip myself."

As it turned out, we did have a lot to lose. Luckily, thanks to my superior powers of observation, disaster was averted. We'd found a potential target, and I was just about to bump into the man, with Carlo poised nearby to make the touch, when I spotted two coppers strolling down the sidewalk. Immediately I backed away from the gent, then skipped over to Carlo. I grabbed his elbow and began steering him through the crowd.

"Hey, what're you doing, Rocco?" Carlo hissed. "Got cold feet?"

"Keep walking. I'll explain later."

When we turned down a side street and the coppers were out of sight, I told Carlo about our close call. He gave a low whistle. "Thanks, Rocco. I might've been caught in the act, and I don't have a bit of fall money put aside."

"What's fall money?" I knew "taking a fall" had something to do with being arrested. I wasn't sure about the money part.

"We call it 'fall money' or 'spring money.' It's money you set aside in case you get pinched. You need ready money to spring you from jail," Carlo said. "Sometimes you can bribe a copper or even make it right with the sucker so he won't press charges."

We walked along for a bit. Carlo's usual smile had vanished. He stopped and put a hand on my arm. When he spoke, I realized he was still thinking about our narrow escape.

"I'm grateful for what you did back there, Rocco," he

said. "Tony has only himself to worry about. He rents a room near Bandits' Roost and can spend just about all his plunder on looking good. It's different for me."

"How do you mean?"

"I got responsibilities. My mother and my sister," Carlo confided. "My mother isn't strong enough to work anymore. She put in so many long hours at the factory when we were little, after my dad died. Bending close over that sewing machine, breathing in all that dust . . . well, it ruined her eyes, broke her health.

"My sister, she's got the same kind of job now, in a sweatshop. She's lucky to bring home five dollars a week. But during slow times, there's no work and she gets nothing. So they depend on me."

I'd never thought much about what Carlo and Tony did when they weren't out on the streets. I wondered if Carlo's mother knew how he made his money. Maybe she was afraid to ask. Or maybe she did know. Maybe she figured they had no other choice.

"Why don't you have fall money put aside, then?" I wanted to know.

"Oh, I imagine Tony has a stash somewhere," Carlo said, rubbing the side of his nose. "And if something bad happened to me, he'd put it up."

"Really?" I raised my eyebrows. I should've stopped there, as Mama often warned, and kept my thoughts to myself. Instead, they spilled out into words.

"Tony sure asks us to trust him a lot," I went on. "I've noticed lately that when he doles out our shares, we never see how much he keeps for himself. And we don't know if he has fall money set aside for either of us."

Carlo stared at me, cocking his head like a quizzical dog. Then he waved my concerns away. "Ah, don't worry about that. Tony would never let us down."

A few days later, after we'd finished a smooth touch and a great meal, Tony put his hand on my arm. Carlo had gone, so it was just the two of us. "We need to have a little talk, kid. I hear you don't trust me."

My face flushed. I could guess what had happened: Carlo had asked Tony about the fall money.

I opened my mouth, but Tony moved his hand to grasp my wrist and held it, hard. "Let's get something straight, Rocco. You're just a little street bandit, nothing more. Don't start putting ideas into Carlo's head when I'm not around. He's part of *my* mob, just like you are. You work for me.

"And you're lucky I took you on. Otherwise, come winter, you'd be sniveling and freezing on the street corners every day, hitting that little triangle of yours and hoping to get a penny."

"Tony, I swear. I didn't mean anything by it," I protested.

"Just watch out," he warned. "You may think you know what you're doing, but you've got a lot to learn."

Did that warning deter me? Did I abandon my plan to continue moll-buzzing on my own? No, reader, I did not. In fact, I did just the opposite.

I became more determined than ever to make use of what I saw as my natural abilities (the heretofore discussed sweet face) to get as much money as I could, as quickly as I could.

Almost every day now, as soon as my midday dinner with Tony and Carlo was over, I'd go scouting on my own, hoping to find another opportunity for moll-buzzing.

And, on a fateful day in late September, I found just what I was looking for.

I was walking back from Wall Street to take up my triangle-banging duties on Mulberry Street when suddenly I noticed a good-looking moll strolling along the sidewalk right in front of me.

I could plainly see the tip of a wallet bulging like a fat, luscious sausage from her pocket. We walked another block. She crossed the street. I crossed behind her.

The crowds were thick around us, but I felt sure I could move so fast no one would notice. With every step, my fingertips itched and burned. I could just feel that leather in my hands; I could imagine heading to my secret alley and stuffing more dollar bills into my hiding spot.

I stuck my hands in my pockets. They popped out again, almost on their own. That leather was so close!

She was a tall young woman, hurrying along, clearly

on her way somewhere. She carried a cloth bag on one shoulder. She'd been to the market stalls; the lacy green tops of a bunch of carrots peeked up out of her bag.

*Maybe she's spent all her money already. Maybe there's nothing left in her wallet.* But her bag wasn't full. Most likely, she was on her way to the baker or butcher. No, this young woman still had money to spend. I could almost smell it.

I was just about to make my move when, from the corner of my eye, I spotted a girl standing at the edge of the street. Something about her made me think of Meddlin' Mary. I looked more closely.

It *was* her! Only this time Mary Hallanan wasn't busy recording the location of a rut in the road or hollering at the driver of a cart.

She was crying.

The Irish girl was standing over a horse in the gutter. If not already dead, the wasted, emaciated animal was surely about to expire. At that moment, Mary looked up, tears staining her cheeks, fists clenched by her sides. For an instant, I thought she recognized me. Then I realized she wasn't seeing me, or anyone.

The look on her face brought me back to the day that had changed everything—to the landlord's yard in Calvello. To that moment when, all because of Old Biter, I'd caught sight of another girl with a face so desperately sad. That girl had been Anna's friend Rosa.

The memory was so strong I must have closed my eyes against it. For the next thing I knew, I tripped, plunging forward. I was so close to the young woman with the wallet—the moll I was about to buzz—that my foot kicked the back of her heel by accident.

She whirled, instantly alarmed, ready to beat off a pickpocket. She was a head taller than me. As she raised her arm, the glimmering gold locket around her neck suddenly swung loose, dangling before my eyes.

It was large and bright, a perfect heart shape on a slender gold chain. I didn't even think. It was more like my baby brother, Vito, reaching out for a sunbeam. In a flash, I grabbed at it. It felt warm and smooth in my hand.

It was instinct—the action of a split second. I didn't mean to steal it. Or did I? I can't say for sure.

Just as I caught the glittering heart, the young woman jerked her head backward.

*Snap!*

The chain broke. The locket was in my hand.

"Stop! Thief!"

Now that I had it, I didn't want to let go. It was gold. It might be worth enough to get me home.

I started to run.


It isn't easy to run on a crowded sidewalk, I can tell you that. I swept around a man with a cane, a woman toting a baby, a peddler selling candies on a tray. I ducked down, then darted a few steps into the road, Mary and the horse behind me now.

The corner. If I could just reach the corner, I could bolt across the street and melt into an alley. I panted. I was a whirlwind of motion, like a runaway cart careening through traffic. People leapt out of my way. They cursed and shouted at me.

I was almost at the corner when I felt someone grab my arm.

*Whack!* He pushed.

*Crash!* I hit the sidewalk, both hands splayed in front of me. My triangle slipped out of my pocket and made a jangling sound on the pavement. But the gold chain was still entwined in my fingers.

The man was big and burly, his face red as a pepper. Still holding tightly to my arm, he pulled me roughly to my feet. He pried the locket out of my hand.

"Gotcha," the man exclaimed, breathing hard. He started marching me off. I turned, meaning to pick up my little musical instrument. It was too late. A small boy darted in and grabbed it. Anything here could be sold for a few pennies.

"You won't squirm out of this one." The man shook me hard. "I caught you red-handed."

He was a copper. I was done for.

# CHAPTER 15

*A long chapter detailing
the dire consequences of the preceding misadventure
and introducing several new personages*

$M$y trial was over in minutes. The copper presented his evidence. The judge asked me a few questions, making himself understood (barely) by sprinkling a few Italian words into his English.

He wanted to know if I had family here in America. I shook my head. He made some marks on a paper. To him, I was just one of hundreds of orphans and homeless children on the streets of the Lower East Side.

The judge didn't inquire about my padrone or seem to notice the scar on my lip. It struck me that people outside of Little Italy probably didn't even know what that brand meant. After all, street kids were always getting into scrapes and had the scars to show for it.

Besides, boys like me were as invisible as you could

get. Most people didn't see the poor, any more than they noticed the broken-down horses pulling streetcars.

*Most people.* But not all. Meddlin' Mary might not see kids like me, yet she did notice everything about those horses. If I hadn't spotted Mary's stricken face that day, I could've easily plucked that moll's wallet. Instead of being arrested, I'd have had more dollars to add to my secret stash in the alley and been further along in my grand scheme to get home.

Mary Hallanan always seemed to bring me trouble.

Eventually someone translated the verdict for me. I was sentenced to a year in the House of Refuge, an institution of reform on Randall's Island. It was, I was told, a place where I'd learn to mend my ways, give up my life of crime, and become a productive member of society.

I had no idea what that meant. Yet I knew one thing: If I was locked up for a year, Papa and Mama wouldn't see a dime from my padrone. And they'd probably think I was dead.

This new chapter in my history began on a blustery day in early October. A policeman rode with me in a cart to a dock near East 118th Street in Harlem, in Upper Manhattan. There he turned me over to an older man with twinkling brown eyes, who led me to a rowboat.

"Let me lean on your shoulder as we get in, there's a good lad," the man said, untying the boat from its mooring. "This knee ain't what it used to be. I'm Officer Reilly from the House of Refuge. Let's get out of this wind and over to Randall's Island, shall we?"

Officer Reilly chattered as we crossed the narrow stretch of water, pointing out all the sights as he rowed. I sat facing him in the boat.

"This here is the Harlem River," he called. "It's not much of a river to speak of, though it is deep enough for small boats to navigate. Randall's Island, where we're headed, is just there to the east. Well, you can see that for yourself, I expect."

I nodded. I even found the corners of my mouth turning up into a smile. I hadn't smiled for a long time, but there was something about Officer Reilly that made me feel better. Maybe it was that he wasn't treating me like a criminal, but like an ordinary boy enjoying a row on the river.

"Bronx Kill!" Officer Reilly jerked one oar to call my attention to the north. "The Bronx is on the other side. Me and my wife live in a nice neighborhood there. Raised two lovely girls, we did."

I smiled again, though I wasn't exactly sure what he was talking about, especially as I remembered that Carlo had once told me "kill" meant to murder. Later, though, I found out that "kill" is an old term for a narrow body of water.

"Now we're coming up to it—this gigantic fortress of a place is the House of Refuge," he went on, pointing at the large brick building close to the shore of the island. It towered over the few trees nearby.

"Big, ain't it?" Seeing my look of horror, he chuckled.

"Aw, lad, it's not that scary. You'll be fine there," he assured me. "Lots of nice boys. Just've had a hard start in life, they have. I imagine it's no different for you, wherever you've come from."

Now that Officer Reilly has started us off, I may as well continue the tour of my new home: the House of Refuge. The whole complex must've been nearly a thousand feet long. The main building, for boys, was indeed enormous, with three big domes and dozens of large arched windows. I later learned it could hold more than four hundred boys. Next to it was a smaller building for girls, though I never went inside it.

The boys' building had dormitories, a chapel, a dining hall, classrooms, a kitchen, a bakery, workshops, and even a hospital. Twice a day, rain or shine, we were sent to an exercise yard behind a great stone wall. In the back were gardens, where in the summer the boys worked at growing vegetables. Near the dock where Officer Reilly and I landed was a storage shed.

Now to the most important part: the food. The meals they gave us weren't nearly as good as Mama's, or even what I'd eaten in restaurants with Tony and Carlo. But at least they fed us regularly. We ate three times a day, which means a lot when you know what it's like to be hungry. We sat at huge long tables; no talking allowed. The daily schedule is still fixed in my brain:

Breakfast (7 a.m.): Bread, molasses, and water
Dinner (noon): Soup, boiled meat, bread, and vegetables
Supper (6 p.m.): Bread, molasses, and water or stew

Notice something missing? No sausages. In fact, for as long as I stayed there, I never even smelled a sausage. Not a one. If you ask me, that alone was reason enough to escape.

But there was one thing we definitely did have an abundance of at the House of Refuge, and that was counting. We stood in line to be counted after we left our morning jobs in the various workshops, where we went to learn a trade. That took place every day between breakfast and the noon meal. Next we were counted after yard time in the afternoon, before we filed into the dining room again. And after supper we were counted as we were marched straight to the dormitories, with their long, straight rows of beds. As I soon discovered, a bed out of line was like a boy out of line—it needed to be straightened.

Lights were out by eight; we were up before seven each morning. Some boys complained they could never get to sleep, what with all the snoring, coughing, and crying that went on. I didn't mind, though. In fact, sleeping was my favorite time of day. Compared with the scratchy, bug-infested straw of 45 Crosby Street, those clean white sheets and iron cot felt wonderful. It was the nicest bed I'd ever slept in.

On my first day, I got my hair clipped and was given a bath. The water turned black as coal and had to be changed three times. My old clothes were taken away and I was issued a pair of pants, a shirt, and a clean gray jacket, a bit worn in the elbows. Plus a new pair of shoes. The ones I'd come with were too small, and I loved being able to wiggle my toes again. The House of Refuge had its own shoemaking operation—I can highly recommend the workmanship.

By then it was late afternoon, and I was turned into the rear yard for fresh air before supper. It was full of other inmates, all wearing gray jackets like mine. I stood uncertainly in the corner alone for a few minutes. Before long, though, I found myself surrounded by three curious boys, who looked to be about fourteen or fifteen.

"Hallo, new kid. What are you in for? Petty grafting?" inquired a stocky lad with fat cheeks, a small nose, and startling blue eyes.

"Moll-buzzing," I admitted, a little embarrassed. "She blew before I could get cleanly off."

The less said about the ill-fated, disastrous episode, the better. Besides, I had no intention of going into details—how seeing Meddlin' Mary's face and that glimmering heart locket had gotten me off balance (in more ways than one). Or how I'd hung my head as the copper marched me off, hoping the horse-loving Irish girl wouldn't catch sight of me.

"You didn't have enough fall money to fix it?" another boy asked. "Or did you get double-crossed by your pals?"

"No, I didn't have any fall money. And . . . and I was working alone."

"Alone?" The first boy raised his eyebrows in surprise. "That's a bold move for a young street bandit."

"Oh, I've done it lots of times," I said smoothly, the lie rolling off my tongue before I could stop myself. I suppose I just wanted to impress them. "Moll-buzzing is my specialty."

"You weren't part of a mob?"

"I was, once. We . . . um . . . we parted ways. I didn't . . . I couldn't trust them."

Should I have trusted Tony? Had he been looking out for me the whole time? Maybe if I *had* listened to him, I wouldn't be locked up now.

When I'd first been put in a cell at the police station on Mulberry Street, I half expected Tony to appear. I thought he might be able to bribe a cop or make it good with the locket girl so she wouldn't press charges.

Yet, as each hour passed, I lost hope. It began to dawn on me that of course Tony and Carlo wouldn't dare come near. Tony had ties with one or two coppers in the neighborhood, and they kept him informed about everything that went on near Bandits' Roost. These same coppers (for a price) might sometimes help convince a victim not to press charges. Not all coppers played this game, though. So Tony wouldn't trust me now. He'd be worried I might finger him and Carlo.

"Trust is important," the fat-cheeked boy was saying. He looked around at the other boys, who gave him a slight nod, as though I'd passed some kind of secret test. He stuck out his hand. "I'm Tommy Brady. Everyone calls me Pug, on account of my nose."

He squished up his face to show me. "See? My auntie gave me the nickname when she heard Queen Victoria loves those silly-looking pug dogs."

I grinned. You couldn't help grinning at Pug.

"Anyhow, if you want to learn the tricks of the grafting trade so you won't get caught, you've come to the right place," he went on. "The House of Refuge is the best school for crime around."

That's how Pug, along with his two friends, George Kercher and Jimmy O'Connor, became my new mob. Jimmy had dark red hair, while George sported a sprinkle of freckles, as though someone had shaken cinnamon across his nose. In a way, they both reminded me of Carlo. Just as Carlo shadowed Tony, George and Jimmy trailed after Pug.

Now that I think about it, I guess Luigi and Marco had been the same. They'd tried to follow me, to look to me for help. But I'd never let them.

"You don't have much to worry about here," George was telling me. "It's better than Sing Sing, which is where you get sent once you turn eighteen. Believe me, you don't want to end up in that prison."

"What happens there?"

"I had a pal in Sing Sing who was put to work ironing

shirts and scorched one by mistake," Jimmy confided. "The guards were sure that he'd done it on purpose, so they beat him with a wooden paddle."

I winced. It sounded just as bad as my padrone's den. "So, that doesn't happen here?"

"Naw," said Pug. "Take my advice: The best thing you can do here is earn the trust of the warden and the guards. They like cooperation and enthusiasm. Do your best to be a model boy. That's the way to get extra privileges."

"What kind of privileges?"

"There's a story that one boy got a job working in the office. They trusted him so much he just opened a drawer, took out a key, and let himself out without anyone batting an eye," Jimmy said, his voiced filled with awe.

"You don't want to get caught trying to escape, though. They'll put you in solitary," George advised. "You'll be locked in a room alone and fed bread and water for a few days. After that, you'll be watched like a hawk and never get another chance to make a break."

"So . . . um . . . do you ever think about escaping?" I asked them.

The House of Refuge might be better than Sing Sing, but I couldn't imagine being locked up for a whole year. I wouldn't even be out for my thirteenth birthday.

"Oh, we want to escape, all right." Pug's smile made his cheeks rise all the way up to his eyes, which peeked out of his face like bright blue buttons. "We just want to do it the right way—so we don't get caught."

I've written this out the way I remember it, but the truth is, my English wasn't so good when I first arrived. So, especially during my first few weeks, it took quite a bit of back-and-forth and gesturing to understand what these boys (who'd all grown up in America and spoke English) were saying and make myself understood in turn.

Tony, Carlo, and I had spoken Italian, except for the English words Carlo had taught me. Carlo's English was actually pretty good, I guess because his sister mixed with lots of Irish girls at her factory. He downplayed this, though, since he never liked to show off in front of Tony.

I was glad to have some American friends to help me learn English. Pug and his mob had a lot to teach me. For it soon became clear that Pug was a bona fide expert in the art of grafting.

"Will you go back to being a pickpocket when you get out, Pug?" I asked one day when we were in the yard for our time in the fresh air.

Fresh air, it seemed, was an essential part of turning us into upstanding young men. I didn't see the point of shivering in the yard when we could be in a warm building. I'd had my fill of being out in rain, sleet, and snow with that little triangle.

"Of course! What else is there in the world to beat grafting?" Pug grinned. "I ain't about to go slave in a factory for pennies a day. That's almost as bad as being walled in here."

"Are you worried about getting caught again?"

"Naw. I just got unlucky," Pug declared. "Your case is different, Rocco. You went out on your own."

Pug's tone became serious. "You've got to have friends you can trust, no matter what. And I'm not just talking about grafting."

I nodded silently. Luigi and Marco had trusted me, even if I hadn't deserved it. They'd be wondering why I disappeared. They probably thought I was dead or had deserted them without a word of farewell. *Maybe Giuseppe will look out for them,* I thought hopefully, though I was pretty sure that wouldn't happen.

I was quiet for so long that Pug leaned close to stare at me, an unaccustomed frown on his face. "You all right there, Rocco?"

"Just thinking."

"Well, don't think too much. You'll hear a lot in here about being good, turning over a new leaf, taking up an honest line of work. Don't let that sort of talk trouble you."

"I won't," I assured him. "I know what I want. I want to bring money home to my parents in Italy. And I don't know how else to do that except by being a pickpocket."

As to whether I was good or bad, it should be quite

apparent to you by now that I was far too muddled to know.

Shortly after arriving at the House of Refuge, I had my first interview with the warden. "You've done a foolish thing . . . um, son," said Warden Sage, staring at a paper on his desk as though trying to find my name.

*How can he keep hundreds of us boys straight?* I wondered. Probably he didn't.

He took off his glasses and rubbed his eyes wearily. "I hope during your time here you will mend your ways. Our mission at the House of Refuge is to show you a new path. We want you to be a productive member of society."

"I am eager to be a good boy, sir," I told him, recalling Pug's advice to get on the good side of the grown-ups in charge. "Uh . . . I'd like to learn more English—maybe even how to read."

I could think of many reasons to get better at the English language. For starters, I'd be able to understand what was being said on the rattlers in case I wanted to ply my trade there. I'd be able to know if someone sitting nearby, for instance, had witnessed the touch and was giving a warning.

"I see." Warden Sage smiled weakly. "We do offer classes part of the day. However, our primary purpose is to train wayward boys for practical jobs in society. I hope you wish to be useful to society?"

"*Sì!* Yes, Warden Sage!" I was taking to heart Pug's advice to be enthusiastic.

"In our workshops, you'll learn a trade you can follow once you're out in the world again," he went on, glancing at the paper again. "Let's see, we have you starting in the shoe shop, blacking shoes."

"Shining shoes?" I wondered how much training that required. I had a flash of myself hard at work as a shoeshine boy on Mulberry Street—and feeling a familiar blocky hand on my shoulder. I could imagine being hauled off by Signor Ancarola to be a street musician again.

Warden Sage cleared his throat. "I suppose if you apply yourself and your conduct is good, you can move to a different workshop."

"Yes, sir." It came out sounding rather sullen.

I cleared my throat and tried again. "Yes, sir! Thank you, sir."

As expected, I did hate blacking shoes, especially for three hours a day. I began to scout around for another workshop. Besides the shoemaking, there was carpentry, baking, and tailoring. But something else caught my eye.

After a few weeks of *swish, swish, swish*ing shoes, I begged my instructor, Mr. Woods, to put in a good word for me with the printshop. Since I'd been following Pug's advice to be a model inmate, Mr. Woods readily agreed.

As it turned out, I enjoyed the printshop even more than I'd expected. It helped me learn English faster and I also made a surprising discovery: The work demanded that I use my mind. I barely knew such jobs existed. Back home, work was physical. Work meant hard labor and sweat.

This was different. Setting type was a kind of puzzle with a rhythm of its own: choosing each letter and putting it into the right place to form words; words coming together to make sentences.

And sentences, I was starting to realize, were just thoughts and ideas made real on paper. I wondered if Giuseppe felt this way about the music he made on his violin—that somehow each little movement of the bow and strings fit together to become something more, something beautiful or happy or sad. Something with meaning.

Mostly, the printing we did was simple. It was practice work, really, mainly notices and signs. I didn't always understand what the words meant, but I tried to be accurate, sounding out each letter in my mind as I set it into place.

Mr. Wright, our instructor, was a thin, balding man who seemed to forget he no longer had hair. He was constantly rubbing his hand over the top of his head, leaving a smudgy trail of ink on its shiny surface. All of us boys who worked for him got ink stains on our shirts too. He kept patting our shoulders to encourage us to continue doing a good job.

"We're at an exciting moment in the history of type," Mr. Wright told us once. "Why, not long ago, the *New York Tribune* became the first newspaper to use a Linotype machine."

"What's that?" someone asked.

"We've got trays of letters here, which we put in place to make words," Mr. Wright explained. "This new invention has a keyboard with ninety characters, which makes it possible to set an entire line of type at one time. Speed is the future, boys, mark my words! Speed!"

Mr. Wright's talk of newspapers reminded me of the papers Carlo and I had waved in our victims' faces. Carlo was always able to convince our suckers they'd be missing out if they didn't read the latest news.

"Mr. Wright, I understand about setting the type, but how do the typesetters know *which* words to put in the paper?" I asked him. "Who tells them what is news?"

He ran a hand over his head, leaving a fresh streak of black ink. I suppose it was a stupid question, yet Mr. Wright didn't seem to mind.

"Reporters, Rocco," he said. "Reporters are the heart of a newspaper. They comb the city looking for news, listening to stories, investigating crimes. Then they describe everything to readers. They write the stories and give them to editors, who make decisions about what's important and which stories go where. Then typeset-ters put the day's stories onto the page."

"Do they teach being a reporter here?" I could already guess the answer.

"No." Mr. Wright laughed. "Boys from the House of Refuge are more likely to be the subject of crime stories than to write them."

# CHAPTER 16

*Showing the sort of insalubrious instruction
provided to inmates at the House of Refuge*

Before proceeding with my narrative, it seems appropriate to provide more details about the real education I and other inmates at the House of Refuge received. Naturally, there were lectures and sermons. But we all learned the most in the yard.

My primary tutor was Pug, a thief so confident and accomplished at the tender age of fifteen that he put even Tony to shame.

"I never worked as a stall, though you might think, given my build, I'd be good at it. But I have quick hands, and by the time I was eleven, I was already a first-class dip," Pug told me.

"That was just the beginning. I'm the oldest of eight, and what I could bring home from picking pockets wasn't quite sufficient to allow Ma to buy bread and milk for my little brothers and sisters. Crikey, they eat a lot! Anyway, once I'd trained Tommy, my next oldest brother, to pick pockets, I moved to doing 'house work.' I became a sneak thief."

"What's that?" We were, as usual, ambling around the exercise yard, trying to keep out of the chill November wind. George and Jimmy had bad colds and were huddled against a storage shed in the corner, beating their arms against their jackets to keep warm.

"I'd go uptown along those fancy streets near Central Park. I'd look for open basements and rummage around for silverware or jewelry," Pug explained. "Always during the day, mind you, not at night, when people are home."

I frowned. "How . . . how would you know where to go—what building to choose?"

"Now, that's the fun part of the whole operation." He grinned and rubbed his palms together. "It worked like this: Me and my pals would head to Coney Island in the summer. We'd find some young servant girls and treat them to ice cream.

"Then we'd get them talking about where they worked and who was home during the day. They never guessed what we were after. And, let me tell you, the plunder was worth it. I had enough to help Ma, and some for me besides."

*Tony would be impressed,* I thought. This was exactly the line of graft he'd like to get into, hobnobbing with pretty maids and eating ice cream cones at Coney Island.

Pug explained that a sneak thief is not the same as a genuine burglar, who operates at night. "Being a burglar is a dangerous undertaking. It takes nerves of steel to break into a house where people are sleeping."

I was pretty sure I couldn't do anything like that. Why, you might get smacked on the head with a candlestick or worse. "You said you got nabbed because of bad luck. Were you caught being a sneak thief?"

"Naw, that was just a simple touch that went wrong," Pug admitted. "It shouldn't have happened, really. I know how to work the system. I had a mouthpiece— a lawyer—with good connections.

"Usually I could fix things up myself before it came to that, especially since I know so many coppers. Just a few months before, right on Grand Street, a copper came up to me and complained that his chief was getting too many complaints about breech-getting on the streetcars."

I knew "breech-getting" was picking men's pockets. "He told you this? So, did he arrest you?"

Pug laughed. "No, I just gave the copper a twenty-dollar bill and he left me and my mob alone."

I whistled. "That's a high price to pay."

He shrugged. Carlo had told me some mobs could earn a hundred dollars a week or more, if they made good touches every day. It was more money than most people ever dreamed of seeing in their lives. I wondered if Pug and his boys had been that good.

Pug scrunched up his eyes then and sighed, as if remembering past triumphs. "No, like I said, in the end I got nailed for the simple act of picking a man's pocket on a streetcar."

"And your fall money didn't help?"

"Not this time. I'd been sent up before the judge once too often," Pug said. "This is my third time here in the House of Refuge."

"It is?"

"Yup. I first darkened these doors when I was ten. And let me tell you something, Rocco. The food hasn't gotten any better."

# CHAPTER 17

*Containing rather a lot,*
*including a heated discussion about the relative*
*merits of going under or over, a nail-biting account*
*of a daring escapade, and a lie*

"The way I see it," said Pug, "we can go under it, or we can go over it. No matter what, the wall stands in our way."

"It's got to be twenty feet high, that wall," whispered George, shooting a quick glance at it.

This was our favorite topic: escape. We were in the yard, getting fresh air, of course. To keep warm, we had to keep walking—fast. We stayed in full view of the guards, and every so often one of us would burst out laughing, pretending to be joking around. No sense in arousing suspicion.

"Look over there in the corner. I bet I could get up that drainpipe at the top," I said, all the while keeping my eyes straight ahead.

Pug snorted. "*You* might, you little monkey, but Jimmy and I are shaped more like round pots of jam."

"Speak for yourself, Pug," protested Jimmy.

"Well, then, what about tunneling under?" I asked Pug.

"Ah, I thought you'd never ask, Rocco," he said, rubbing his hands together. "See that shed over there, next to the wall? That's where garden tools are kept."

"This past summer, we grew tomatoes as big as baseballs," George put in. "Mine were the biggest. Red as sunsets."

"Crikey, George! You've got to concentrate," Pug admonished. "We're not thinking about tomatoes now."

"Yeah," said Jimmy, beating his arms to stay warm. "Next thing we take out of that shed won't be a hoe— it'll be a snow shovel."

"If we do things right, none of us will be here to shovel snow, let alone eat Randall's Island tomatoes next summer," Pug said softly. "We'll be free. Because there are three very important things about that old shed. Can you guess what they are, Rocco?"

"It's close to the wall," I offered.

"What else?"

"Um . . . it's got shovels in it."

"Very good," said Pug with a nod of approval. "And the last thing?"

I shook my head. I wanted to impress Pug, but I couldn't think of anything else. Then all at once I remembered Signor Ferri's stable in Calvello. "I know! I bet it has a dirt floor we can dig a hole in."

"You've got it, young Rocco!" Pug slapped me on the back, and my face flushed with pleasure. It felt good to be part of a new mob.

Pug outlined our plan a few days later. It had two parts. As I'd hoped, we would tunnel under the wall. The first step would be to break the lock to the shed. We'd accomplish that during our morning time in the yard.

"Just like with picking pockets, we'll need a distraction," Pug announced. We nodded. We all knew the importance of distractions.

The second part of the plan called for a couple of us to slip into the shed and begin digging a tunnel. We'd do that during each yard break for as long as it took.

"What if it takes us more than a day or two?" I wondered. "Won't someone notice that the lock is broken?"

"Look around you, Rocco," Pug said, waving his hand. "In this weather, the guards are happy to stay close together against the main building. They don't want to be out here any more than we do."

"Besides," put in George. "We can break the lock but put it back so it looks untouched. Unless it snows, no one goes near that shed this time of year. It shouldn't be hard for one or two of us to slip in."

"What then?" I wanted to know. "What do we do once we finish the tunnel and get under the wall? How do we get off the island?"

"That's simple. We run to the water," said Pug. "Then we jump in and swim."

"Swim?"

"It ain't far," Jimmy assured me.

I swallowed hard. I hadn't thought about that part. "It's November. Won't the water be freezing?"

"It's not for long," Pug said confidently. "You *can* swim, can't you, Rocco?"

I nodded. "Of course I can swim."

And, of course, I was lying.

The shed break-in was planned for two weeks later, on Thanksgiving Day, which, the boys told me, was an American holiday.

"They feed us an extra big dinner, and there'll be fewer guards on duty," Pug explained. "Guards don't like to work that day, so there's always a few who just don't show up." Pug's past experiences always came in handy.

On the appointed day, Pug and Jimmy went to lean against the shed. Pug bent down, idly fiddling with one shoe, minding his own business. In reality, he was taking out a sharp stone he'd managed to find and slip inside his shoe for safekeeping.

At the same moment, on the opposite side of the yard, George started a ruckus. He was a sharp lad, that George. He didn't do anything as obvious as yelling or picking on someone. Instead, he grabbed some pebbles and, from behind one of the most notorious bullies in the yard, began pitching them at a group of boys.

Then he crossed the yard to join Pug while the shouting match he left behind ignited into a fistfight. The guards ran over to stop it. Pug was already in the shed by then, having broken the lock with the stone.

Jimmy was also inside, then George slipped in too. I had been assigned to stay on guard and had even brought a book with me. I leaned against the door of the shed, pretending to read.

To make this more believable, I'd been carrying a book in the yard each day for a week. I still wasn't able to actually read an entire page, but thanks to my work in the printshop, I was beginning to make more sense of letters and words.

When the bell rang to signal the end of yard time, I banged my heel against the wall of the shed. Then, when I was sure no guard was looking our way, I kicked again to let my mob know that the coast was clear. They emerged, grinning, one by one.

As we filed back inside, Pug whispered, "The ground is hard. But I expect that in two days of digging—maybe three—we'll have it done."

It took a full three days, and with each one that passed, I got more nervous we'd be found out. I kept fearing that a guard would decide to take a stroll around the yard and notice the broken lock. But no one did. Or what if it snowed? Luckily, the weather held.

The day of the break was cold and gray, with dark,

threatening clouds filling the sky. Just as I'd been doing all along, I brought a book to the yard and took up my position against the shed, my head bowed over a page.

Pug disappeared inside. Then George, and finally Jimmy. All I had to do was follow them.

I didn't.

*Why?* you may be asking. These were the members of my mob. We had hatched the scheme together. They were, I knew, waiting anxiously for me on the other side of the stone wall.

The reason was simple: I was too frightened to face that cold, dark water. I could almost feel it closing over my head, the sensation of my shoes pulling me to the bottom.

"Of course I can swim," I'd told Pug. I'd never even been near water.


"Coward," Pug hissed.

It was more than a week later. We were heading down the corridor for breakfast when, in a flash, he pulled me around a corner and pushed me into a small broom closet before any guard could notice.

My heart thumped like crazy. I swallowed hard. Goose bumps of fear prickled my arms. I knew what was coming.

Because they hadn't made it. Barely an hour after they had escaped, Pug, Jimmy, and George were all captured, picked up as they tried to swim the Bronx Kill.

They'd been spotted as they ran across the open fields to the water. The three had reached the water just fine, but before they were halfway across, they had been pulled into boats and brought back.

Then they'd spent the next six days on bread-and-water rations in solitary confinement (or, in the case of George, a hospital bed, on account of he swallowed so much icy water he couldn't stop shivering).

I couldn't meet Pug's eyes. I hung my head and was silent. I felt almost as scared as I had the day of the break.

Pug pushed my shoulders up against the wall. My head jerked backward and hit the hard surface with a thwack. "Ow!"

"So did you? Jimmy doesn't believe that you did, but I'm not so sure."

"Did I what?" I was stalling. I knew what he wanted to know.

"Did you rat on us? Did you lead the guards to us?" He shook me so hard my head rocked back and forth, making drumbeats on the wall. His thumbs dug into my shoulders, and I could feel tears start up.

"N-no!" I stammered. "I swear it!"

"What happened, then? Why didn't you come with us?"

"I don't know. . . ." I tried to shrug, but with his hands gripping my shoulders, I couldn't move. I was too scared to budge.

"I—I didn't w-want to admit it," I managed to stammer. "It's just that . . . I—I can't swim . . . all that well."

Suddenly he let go and sputtered, "You little snake. You can't swim at all, can you? Yet you let us waste valuable minutes waiting for you to come through the tunnel. You lied!

"We had a chance, Rocco. The best chance I've had." Pug's voice was cold and hard. "But because I'm loyal, because I believed in you, trusted you, I lost it."

"Can . . . can you try again?"

He cuffed me on the side of my face. "You don't have the right to ask that anymore. I don't want to ever talk to you again. Stay away from Jimmy and George too—from all of us. Understand?"

"I'm sorry," I whispered.

Pug didn't hear. He was gone, stomping off down the hall to join the line of boys for breakfast.

I *was* sorry—sorry to have lost my only friends there, boys who knew more than me. And I was sorry to have lost my place in another mob.


I didn't talk to Pug, George, or Jimmy again. I didn't make other friends either. Pug passed the word: I was a liar and a coward. I was not to be trusted.

Once, in the yard, Jimmy made eye contact and gave me a half smile, but Pug caught him at it and jabbed him in the ribs with his elbow.

No one else spoke to me unless they had to—not in the yard, in the printshop, or in the dormitory at night. I spent most of my time puzzling out the words in books, keeping my face hidden. I didn't cry, though sometimes I came close. And now I really did bring a book to the yard to have something to do.

The guards and warden noticed the way I was being treated. I expect Warden Sage put out the word that I was so virtuous I'd refused to take part in the escape attempt. Mr. Wright was extra nice. Whenever he saw me, Officer Reilly winked, patted my head, and slipped me a lemon drop.

I was indeed sorry to lose my friends. But, in the end, I reaped an unexpected benefit from the whole unfortunate episode: escape.

# BOOK THREE

*Spring 1888*

# CHAPTER 18

*Being very full of daring
(but once again disreputable) acts*

Christmas had come and gone: my first Christmas away from home. Someone set up a small Nativity scene made of rough clay figures in the House of Refuge's chapel. It was hard to tell the donkeys from the goats, which made me think inmates had probably made them.

Even the singing and some special pudding couldn't lift my spirits. Everything felt hollow compared to my memories of home, where the whole town celebrated together. I knew Papa, Mama, Anna, Emilia, and Vito would all be at the living Nativity scene on Christmas Eve. It was one of our biggest festivals.

Each year, a woman and a man dressed as Mary and Joseph would appear at the outskirts of town with a donkey. Neighbors would follow them as the couple walked through the town, knocking on doors and being turned away. Finally, the procession ended at the church. There, before the crib with an image of the baby Jesus, people would make offerings of food.

Emilia and Anna had helped Mama bake bread last year for our family's gift. I remember how Emilia had started scratching her head with her hands covered with flour. Like Mr. Wright walking around with black marks on his head, my little sister had ended up with white streaks in her glossy dark hair. I wondered if she would do the same thing this year.

Last Christmas, the night had been still and the streets quiet except for the sound of voices lifted in song inside the church. I'd been in charge of choosing one of Signor Ferri's donkeys for the procession and making sure the animal got back to the stable again. As you can probably guess, I didn't choose Old Biter.

Now it was March. Since the attempted escape, I'd continued to be a model boy. I'd applied myself in the printshop and the schoolroom. I didn't get into fights or cause trouble. No matter who teased and tormented me, I kept my eyes down without rising to the bait. I barely spoke. That wasn't always easy. Sometimes I had to fold my hands into fists, digging the tips of my nails into my palms until I made marks.

It also meant that since I couldn't practice my English with my fellow inmates, I had to talk instead to the warden and guards. Since it was a bit unusual for someone like me—an ignorant immigrant delinquent (as I am sure they considered me)—to make so much progress in English, I soon got the reputation of being a wonderful specimen of a reformed boy.

One day, Warden Sage sent for me to come from the classroom to his office. I arrived to find a gentleman and two fine ladies, perched on their chairs like colorful pieces of fruit on display.

"Ah, here's the boy I mentioned. Come, Rocco, don't be shy." Warden Sage waved me in.

I went to where he stood beside his desk and presented myself, posture erect as a soldier's. We'd recently been doing drills to give us military discipline. So, for good measure, I saluted.

One lady oohed and aahed at that, bringing her gloved hands together in a dainty clap. "Isn't he just darling? Look at those cheeks."

"Rocco, these good citizens have come to inspect the House of Refuge and learn about our work," Warden Sage explained. "Tell them how you like it and what you have learned in your time here."

I beamed at the visitors and spoke slowly and clearly. "I am learning the printing trade. Also, the teachers are helping me to speak and write English."

"What were you doing before you came here, young man?" asked the other lady, who wore a purple hat that looked to me like a bunch of grapes stuck on her head.

I hung my head, as though barely able to think about

my horrible past. "I had fallen in with some older boys, ma'am, who set me on a path to wickedness and stealing. I was arrested for pinching a moll's leather . . . um, that is to say, for attempting to steal a lady's purse."

This seemed a good point to wipe my eyes, so I did that. I added, "Thanks to the House of Refuge, I realize what I did was wrong. Now I am set on the path to honesty and virtue."

It was such a good performance I think even Warden Sage believed me. I fit the role of reformed rascal quite well. But I still looked rather pathetic. Even with more food, my arms and legs stuck out like bony sticks in my growing body. And, of course, there was my sweet face, which had gotten me into so much trouble.

March was warm that year. One Saturday afternoon, about a year since I'd come to America, the air was so pleasant we walked in the yard in our shirtsleeves. I overheard some guards talking about getting the garden started sooner than usual, since it seemed we could expect an early spring.

Everyone in the group of men nodded except Officer Reilly, my old friend. He claimed he could tell the weather by the pain in his bad right knee. "Don't count on these warm days to last. My knee don't agree with you."

The next day, after chapel, Officer Reilly pulled me out of line and slipped me a lemon drop as usual. "Young

Rocco, I've got an errand to run first, but when I get back, I'm going to need a hand down at the dock after the midday dinner.

"My knee's telling me we got some bad weather coming, and I want all our boats and equipment lashed down well so nothin' blows away. Think you can help me out?"

I nodded. "Yes, sir."

"I'm shorthanded because it's Sunday and so my regular helper is off," he added. "Just meet me at the back door at one and I'll sign you out and we'll go down to the dock."

"I'll be there on time," I promised. "Sir, do you think we have a lot of rain coming?"

"Forecast said maybe a little rain later. I don't know about them weather forecasters, though." He grimaced as he started hobbling down the corridor. "All I can say is, something's coming. My knee ain't hurt like this all winter. And I'll trust my knee anytime."

All through our dinner of boiled cabbage and potatoes with little dried-up bits of corned beef mixed in, my mind raced. I looked at the limp green slice of cabbage on my fork and realized my hand was shaking with excitement.

Alone with Officer Reilly near the dock on a Sunday afternoon: This was my chance.

Officer Reilly was my favorite guard. I'd gotten to know him pretty well over the past few months, ever since the day he'd brought me to Randall's Island. I helped him carry things, because of his bad knee.

Sometimes I asked questions about his life. He often talked about his wife and two grown daughters. One was about to have a baby, he boasted with pride.

"Never thought I'd be a grandpa," he chuckled. "I'll tell you this, Rocco, though I know you won't believe me. It all goes by in a flash, and the good times, they go twice as fast as the bad."

Now I caught sight of Pug across the room and quickly looked down at my plate. Pug had never forgiven me. In my place, Pug would probably think nothing of banging poor old Officer Reilly over the head with a shovel if it meant getting away.

I felt a twinge of guilt as I plotted to betray Officer Reilly's trust. But I was about to do it anyway.


After the meal, I met Officer Reilly at the back door. He signed me out with the guard there, and we made our way down to the shed near the dock. A rowboat and a larger launch bobbed in the water nearby.

"This launch is brand-new and has one of those grand-father clock engines they just invented in Germany," he said. "Was quite a feat to get one here. Do you like en-gines? This one is a beauty."

I didn't know anything about engines and struggled to come up with an intelligent question. "So, um . . . the engine makes the boat go faster than rowing?"

"That it does, son!" He clapped me on the back.

"Why, it has a one-cylinder, one-horsepower engine. I hear they've got a two-horsepower engine being tested out over in Germany. I read all about it. Fellers named Daimler and Maybach invented it. I tell you, the world is changing fast, which is why you don't want to spend your life in prison, boy."

"No, I certainly don't, sir."

He was right about that. I studied the strip of water on the west side of the island. It was called a river, but it wasn't much wider than a canal. Right now the water was dark and churned up by a strong breeze.

Above us, the skies were boiling with black, gloomy clouds. It hadn't started to rain yet, but it looked like it might at any second. I shivered. I was glad my plan included taking a boat. Just a few minutes in the water would be the end of me, even if I could swim.

"So, we're going to take the engine out of the boat?" I asked.

"Yup. We'll put it in the shed. I used the launch this morning to carry over a visitor for Warden Sage. Why, we skimmed over those six hundred feet of water like a shot. Plus, it's a lot easier on my old joints than rowing.

"I just came back from dropping the visitor off at the pier at One Hundred Eighteenth Street," he went on. "Now's the time to store the engine nice and dry before the storm hits. Would've done it myself already, except for my bad knee. I like to have help carrying it up to the shed."

Officer Reilly unlocked the shed door. The wind caught it, whipping it out of his hand. "Whoa! We're in store for a gale. Rocco, grab that rock there to prop the door open while we go for the engine."

I did so and then followed him down to the dock, where the launch and rowboat made a steady rhythm as they strained against their ropes and bumped against the wooden dock.

"Gentle," he warned as we lifted the engine out of the launch. He had to shout a little over the wind. "Now let's get 'er into the shed. I got a special place all set up on my workbench there. Want to give 'er a good cleaning."

We walked carefully up the bank and into the shed and then set the engine down.

"Close the door, lad, will you? That gust is blowing right on my neck," said Officer Reilly, not looking at me. Already he couldn't wait to begin cleaning the engine.

This was it. "Should I . . . should I bring up the oars from the rowboat now, sir?"

"Oh yeah, yeah. That's a good idea, go on, then. You're a fine lad," he said absently, grabbing a cloth and leaning close to examine some tiny part of the precious engine.

Too absently. Officer Reilly *trusted* me. And I was about to let him down.

I was shaking inside as I went back down to the dock. *I can still make a different choice,* I thought. *I can bring the oars up to the shed, put them away, and sleep in a real bed tonight. I can do the rest of my time—seven more months—and keep going to school and learning a trade.*

Why didn't I make that choice? You may well be shaking your head by now. The sensible thing would have been to give up my attempt, especially with those dark, threatening clouds swirling overhead.

Not only that, but it might have been the best thing for my future. Maybe I *could* have gotten apprenticed to a printer or gotten some other kind of honest job. I guess I was just too muddled to see it.

I went back to the shed, opened the door, and made some noise in a pile of wood in the corner. Officer Reilly still had his back to me, bent happily over his engine.

"Done!" I called cheerily. "I'll just run up and sign myself back in."

"Oh, all right. Save me the trouble. That's a good lad," he said again, intent on getting the last specks of dirt out of his pride and joy.

It was, of course, against the rules for me to return alone.

I had to hope that the rules had slipped Officer Reilly's mind. Because while he thought me safely back in the House of Refuge, I'd be rowing myself across the water.

Even if he did look up and see that I hadn't actually brought the oars in, his bad knee meant I'd still have time to get a head start.

I ran to the rowboat and untied it quickly. Then I held it steady in the rocking water while I clambered in. The shed door stayed closed, and no one else was in sight.

The boat spun away from the dock, and for a second I panicked. The wind was high, whipping around the rowboat so I almost couldn't control it. I'd never rowed before. I had seen it done, though, and after spinning in circles a couple of times, I managed to get myself pointed in the right direction.

"Crikey!" I exclaimed, using Pug's favorite expression. This was harder than it looked.

Officer Reilly had said the distance was about six hundred feet. I pulled hard on the oars. I was almost halfway across, rowing with my back facing Manhattan, when the door of the shed flung open. Officer Reilly appeared in the doorway, waving his arms frantically.

He cupped his hands around his mouth and shouted. I couldn't catch it at first. And then I was almost sure I hadn't heard right. Because what I thought I heard didn't make too much sense given the springlike weather we'd been having—or for someone yelling at an escaping inmate.

What he yelled was this: "Come back, Rocco! My knee tells me it's gonna snow hard!"

# CHAPTER 19

*Containing a storm so terrible that the reader cannot laugh even once through the entire chapter*

Poor Officer Reilly!

He'd been taken in. Taken in by my innocent face and polite speech. He didn't realize how well Tony had trained me to fool a sucker. I hoped he wouldn't get into trouble because of me. After all, boys tried to escape all the time.

Most, like Pug, George, and Jimmy, didn't make it. Around Christmas, a boy in my dormitory had tried to go over the wall, but broke his leg jumping off on the other side. Pug had told us about an inmate who managed to swim across the Bronx Kill. A week later, he made the mistake of visiting an old friend who'd been arrested. In the police station, a copper overheard him bragging to his friend about his daring escape. He was nabbed right then and there.

No one, though, had ever done what I was attempting: to get away in the midst of a ferocious storm. The strong gusts almost blew my cap away, and I had to try to stuff it in my pocket without letting go of the oars. The water was dark and wild. It started to sprinkle, but those clouds looked so heavy I felt sure they would burst over my head anytime now. And it didn't help that I had no idea how to row a boat and keep it pointed in the right direction—away from the House of Refuge.

But I did it. By the time I reached the dock on the Manhattan side of the Harlem River, my hands and face stung with cold, though at least I still felt a little warm from my struggle to get across.

Luckily, no one saw me tie up the boat. I stashed the oars inside, hoping they wouldn't be stolen. That would just make Officer Reilly more upset. As I walked away from the wharf, I considered getting rid of my telltale House of Refuge gray coat. But the wind was too fierce. Besides, I figured it wouldn't be noticed on such a stormy Sunday.

I'd landed at the pier at 118th Street. By the time I walked over to Fifth Avenue, the sprinkles had turned to light rain and the light rain had become a downpour. My plan was to walk south along the east boundary of Central Park and head toward Little Italy. I was more than a hundred and thirty blocks—seven miles, I guessed—from the alley near Mulberry and Hester Streets where I'd hidden my four dollars.

At least, I wasn't worried about getting lost. Even though New York City is enormous, it's easy to find your way around because it's laid out like a grid. Numbered streets run horizontally across the island, east to west. The lower numbers are in the southern part. The avenues run up and down, north to south. The blocks between the avenues take longer to walk across since they're much wider.

(If you've been here yourself, you'll know what I'm talking about. In any case, for your edification, I've included a map at the end of this history, so this may be a good time to peruse it. I drew it myself, so it's a bit rough, but at least you'll get a feel for the lay of the land.)

I kept heading south, and before long I reached the northeast corner of Central Park, at 110th Street and Fifth Avenue. I considered sleeping in the park under some rock or bush, but the thought of my hidden stash of money and a roof over my head kept me moving. I knew of lodging houses where you could rent a bunk with a locker for fifteen cents. For twenty-five cents, you could even get a tiny room to yourself.

But I wanted to make my money last as long as I could. I'd head for a place Carlo had once pointed out to me: Happy Jack's Canvas Place, on Pell Street, where for seven cents you could sleep on a strip of canvas that was hung like a hammock. That would be just fine for me. I put my head down and kept on.

The wind and rain battered me from all sides, slashing my skin like needles. My hair felt as heavy as a cold, soaked rag. It was hard to keep my eyes open without being stung by raindrops, so at first I almost didn't notice the copper up ahead. Quickly I stepped inside a doorway and waited for him to turn the corner, shaking my head like a dog.

I hadn't wanted to go through Central Park; it was so enormous I was afraid I'd get lost. Now I wondered if I might be safer there than on the streets. Getting turned around and losing time was a risk I'd have to take. I didn't want a copper noticing my coat and asking me any questions.

A little farther along, I found an entrance and followed a walking path into Central Park. Around me, giant trees swayed. Their bare branches screeched and clicked above me. I imagined them as giants fighting with each other. Whenever there was a big *crack!* I jumped, afraid some tremendous limb might fall on my head.

My socks and shoes were soaked through; my pants clung to my legs. I couldn't stop shivering; it was as if I was shaking from the inside out. All at once I remembered I'd stuffed my cap in my pocket. *Stupid!* I should've thought of that sooner. I dragged it out with red, shaking fingers and pulled the brim down low. At least now I could see a little better.

But what I saw frightened me. Central Park was so wild—bushes bending in the wind, tree branches knocking overhead, rivulets of water streaming down hills and making giant puddles on the walkways. In all the months I'd been in America—in my whole life—I'd never been alone in a storm like this. Every so often, I caught sight of one or two people in the distance, but they always had their heads down. As the afternoon wore on, I saw fewer people. Everyone had fled to the safety of home.

Everyone but me. I pressed on, step by step, head down, placing one foot in front of the other. I tried to stay on paths close to Fifth Avenue, on the east side of the park. Sometimes, with so many twists and turns, I got turned around. I just did my best to keep heading south. Whenever I realized I was walking in circles, I stopped, got my bearings, and started out again.

I lost track of time. It seemed like hours before I came to the boundary wall. I had made it through the whole park! But this corner didn't look familiar. It wasn't where I'd come in last summer with Tony and Carlo. I walked to the sidewalk and looked up at the street sign: Seventh Avenue, two wide blocks west of where I'd started. I had crossed the park from east to west.

It would take me longer now since I'd gone out of my way. *It's all right,* I told myself as I passed the corner of Fifty-Eighth Street and Seventh Avenue. My destination was still more than sixty blocks away. In good weather, it might take me less than two hours of walking. Now? I had no idea. I would just follow Seventh Avenue down for a while, then cut over on Bleecker Street to the Lower East Side. At least, I hadn't gotten completely lost—or been knocked down by a falling branch.

I plodded on. It was late afternoon and colder than ever. I was no longer worried about being spotted: I'd never seen the streets of New York so deserted.

Then, suddenly, everything changed. All at once the ground seemed to slide out from under me. *Whoosh!* In a second, I was flat on my back, slammed against the sidewalk.

Ice! The rain had become sleet, making the ground slick and slippery. Drops of frozen rain slashed at my face like my padrone's sharp knife. I got to all fours, then slowly to my feet, trying to balance as best I could. I tested the pavement, moving one foot out slowly. Cautiously feeling my way along the sides of buildings wherever I could, I slid along. At this rate, it would take me hours to get to Mulberry Street.

This really *wasn't* like any storm I'd ever seen. It was something else entirely. It was dangerous. *I could die out here,* I realized. I *would* die if it got much colder, if I stopped moving, or if I fell and hit my head. I could imagine myself lying alone in the gutter, just like a forgotten cart horse.

That thought scared me. I felt a sob catch in my

throat. I shook my head hard. I wouldn't cry. I hadn't, not once, not even when Signor Ancarola flashed his silver knife. Besides, crying wouldn't help. There was no one around to hear me.

I took a long, shuddering breath to steady myself. The image of Old Biter popped into my mind. I imagined him plodding steadily behind me. *Clop clop, clop clop.*

I would be like Old Biter. I wouldn't let this storm frighten me. One breath, one step. Left, right. My heart stopped racing. I was still miserable and shivering, but the panic slipped away.

And that's how it went. The wind attacked me ferociously, as if it wanted to pick me up and throw me down again. But I managed to shuffle slowly along, inch by inch, foot by foot. Forty-Fourth, Thirtieth, Twenty-Sixth. The street signs kept me going.

The gas lamps barely glowed as the darkness deepened. With my head bent low, I almost bumped into a telegraph pole. Clinging to the pole to rest for a minute, I calculated my route. I was still on Seventh Avenue, just below Fourteenth Street. I would stay on Seventh for about ten more blocks, then in Greenwich Village take a left on Bleecker Street to head east, back across town, and finally down to Little Italy. *I can do this,* I told myself.

I let go of the pole and ventured carefully forward

again, my feet making a sort of *swish, swish* rhythm on the icy sidewalk. It was all so slow! I hadn't gotten far when I caught the sound of a voice behind me.

*Is someone hollering?* I turned my head.

*It can't be true!*

But it was. Even in the gloom and the sleet, I knew that red scarf, that clear, strong voice, those urgent, waving arms.

Meddlin' Mary.

And, as usual, Mary Hallanan was hollering. This time she was hollering at me.

# CHAPTER 20

*A surprising instance of my rising to the occasion*

"Hallo there! Can you hear me? Come back!"

Of course it was the crazy Irish girl. Who else would be out in this weather?

I hesitated. I was, after all, an escaped inmate. I couldn't take the risk of talking to people. Maybe I could pretend I hadn't seen her, that I hadn't heard her voice.

"Help! I need help! Horses! My father!"

*Her father.* That would make talking to her even more dangerous. Any grown-up would be likely to turn me in.

"Please," she cried, cupping her hands around her mouth to be heard, "my father's hurt!"

Out of the blue, a thought came to me: If my sisters, Anna or Emilia, were somewhere stranded in a storm,

I'd want someone to help them. If Papa was hurt in an accident in the field, I'd want someone to bring him home safely.

This was Meddlin' Mary, who wouldn't walk away from an animal in need. I *couldn't* leave her. I heaved a big sigh and turned around.

Mary shuffled to meet me, grabbing at my arm for balance. The wind tore her words to shreds. "Oh, thank you. Thank you! I was afraid you couldn't hear me at first. They're just a little ways over here on Fourteenth Street. I was getting so scared."

Her feet slipped. She flailed, she lunged, she pulled me down with her. We both tumbled hard to the icy ground. Slush covered my hands.

"Hey!" I sputtered.

"Sorry!" Mary was on her feet first. She didn't have gloves on either. She grabbed my hand and pulled me up. "Gosh, your hand is cold. Why did you fall? You were supposed to hold me up!"

*Me?* I was already regretting my decision.

We crept along icy Fourteenth Street until, up ahead, I saw our destination. An empty omnibus stood deserted on the side of the street, two horses still in the traces. Nearby, a burly man of about forty leaned against a building, head bowed, half bent over as if in pain.

"One of the mares reared," Mary began, talking so quickly I could barely follow. "Da fell backward and twisted his ankle bad. He got the wind knocked out of him and couldn't breathe for a minute or two. He could have cracked his head! The driver took off—said he'd come for the horses later. Understand?"

I shook my head, confused. *Wind? Knocked? Driver?* It was as if she had started in the middle of some story. What did she want?

When I didn't answer, she pinched the skin of my wrist—hard. "Are you stupid?"

I yelped and turned to her. Her cheeks were red and chapped from the wind. Her dark hair was half tucked up inside a knit cap, though curly tendrils stuck out all over. "Do you understand English?"

"Yes!" I spat through chattering teeth. It was the first word I'd spoken since leaving Officer Reilly. "I . . . I just . . . What do you want me to do?"

"Help Da unhitch the horses, of course." She rolled her eyes, then leaned close again to yell in my ear. "We need to get them home to Barrow Street. It's too dangerous for Da to ride. The horses might not even be used to a rider. Da will have to limp along.

"I just hope his ankle isn't broken," she added. She slipped and almost pulled me down again. This time I was ready. I planted my feet and kept her steady. Our faces came close and our eyes met.

I was afraid for a second she might recognize me as the boy she'd pelted with snowballs a year ago. Or maybe she'd remember seeing me get arrested for stealing the locket. Maybe she'd guess I was a runaway.

But no. Mary wouldn't remember one boy.

"We need to go to Nine Barrow Street. It's only ten blocks or so." Mary was hollering again. *Even a ferocious storm can't keep her from chattering,* I thought. Her eyes and cheeks were red, and not just from the wind and sleet. She'd been crying too.

"Oh, this is all *my* fault! We shouldn't have gone out. We . . . well, I *really* wanted to say goodbye to Mr. Bergh," she said with a shaky breath. "I made Da take me. Mr. Bergh . . . he's so ill. They say he's dying. I know he's old, but . . . I don't like it when people die. He lives at Fifth Avenue and Thirty-Eighth, but it's taken us hours to walk back. Hours!

"Then we came across the driver and this omnibus. If we hadn't come out, we wouldn't have found the horses, so I suppose that's good, isn't it? The poor horses. I don't blame the mare for rearing—all this garbage blowing around. That scares them, you know.

"The driver threw up his hands and walked away. Said he was done in and they could die for all he cared," she babbled on. I could barely catch her words in the wind. "I bet he'll come to the stable looking for them later. And won't give a thought to how we got them there—or that my da got hurt after he abandoned his own horses."

Her voice rose, and I sensed she was on the edge of panic. I grasped her arm. I found myself saying, "It'll be all right. We can do it. I'm strong. Your father can lean on me."

I saw tears start in her eyes. She *was* scared. "Oh, thank you. I'm Mary Hallanan. What's your name?"

Now, this was when I should have lied, I suppose. Instead, I just blurted out my name. "Rocco. Rocco Zaccaro."

Then I said again, "It will be all right. We can do it."

And why not?

After all, I'd already stolen a boat, escaped across a river, and walked miles through a wild and icy Central Park. Getting an injured man and a couple of horses home should be easy.

When we reached Mary's father, she pointed at me. "Da, this is Rocco. He can help."

Mr. Hallanan straightened up and reached out to shake my hand. "Good lad. Well, what do you think will work here? I got to admit that fall has addled my brains a bit."

He was asking me for my opinion! If a grown man needed my help, that meant he might be suffering from cold and shock. Back home in Calvello, Mama had occasionally treated men who'd been hurt, usually in the fields, or sometimes in fights. I knew pain could make it hard to think straight. And I also knew just what we should do.

"Sir, if you lean on me, you can unhitch the horses safely. Mary can lead one horse," I suggested. "And we'll follow. I can support you so you don't have to put much weight on your leg."

"Good plan." Mr. Hallanan nodded. "I'm not stopping till I've got my feet up by the fire and a cup of hot tea and brandy in my hand."

Putting an arm over my shoulder, he braced himself against me. I tried to be as steady as I could, though he was quite a bit heavier than me. He took a deep breath and tested his right leg, wincing as he did. "Now, laddie, let's move to the horses, slow and steady."

He groaned with every step, yet his fingers were sure as he unharnessed the horses. Even hurt, he was probably faster than either Mary or I would've been. The animals seemed to accept his gentle touch now, though they shifted their feet whenever a hard blast of wind hit them. They were nervous and restless, their eyes wide and frightened.

Mary stood nearby so her father could hand the reins of the first horse to her. "Careful as you go, lass. We'll be right behind you."

She nodded, her attention already on the horse. We got the second horse free and were soon following her, back along Fourteenth Street to the corner of Seventh Avenue.

"Steady, girl!" Mr. Hallanan called to our mare.

Then he bent down and said in my ear, "Dratted ice! Let's hope she doesn't go down and bring us with her. I swear, if it's the last thing I do, I'm gonna work on those rubber horseshoe pads I told Mr. Bergh about."

The warmth of moving and the relief of heading home seemed to have revived him. The sleet and wind were fierce, but now he was talking too, and began to tell me about his idea for an invention to help keep horses safe on ice. *Mary must get her love of gab from her father,* I thought. Every time I'd seen Mary she was talking or, sometimes, yelling. I didn't know how they were even speaking. By now every muscle in my body felt tense, my teeth were chattering, and my lips were numb.

We'd never had long conversations at home, though Mama liked to sing while she cooked. Not Papa. I used to walk beside him to the fields each morning. Most days, we wouldn't say ten words to each other.

Mary Hallanan seemed so fond of talking she barely noticed whether the person next to her understood a thing she said. And now here was her father, blathering on about some sort of shoe made of rubber—whatever that might be—when so far as I could tell, we might die before we got warm again.

Just ten blocks or so. It felt like miles. We stayed close behind Mary, who kept a slow but steady pace, stopping often to turn and yell, "Are you all right, Da? Almost there."

I sensed a change in the sleet that slashed at me. The drops became smaller, icier.

*It's not stopping,* I realized. *Officer Reilly was right. This is all about to change to snow.*

At last, Mary turned into Barrow Street. Mr. Hallanan threw up his free hand to point. "That's it. Follow Mary

through the archway under the sign: MICHAEL HALLA-
NAN BOARDING AND STABLE. Designed the blacksmith
shop and stable myself, I did."

Then the horses' hooves were clopping on the brick
walkway that led from the street to the rear. Under
cover of the arch overhead, Mr. Hallanan stopped, removed his hat, and shook the ice from it.

"Rocco, was it? You can stay tonight," he said. "I've got
a cot out back for Tim, my stableboy. He's at home with
his family since it's Sunday. We'll soon get the horses
brushed and fed, and some hot soup in our own bellies."

He touched my coat and looked into my face. Our
eyes met. His voice was quiet. "You'll be safe with us,
lad."

*He knows!* I thought. *Somehow, he knows. But how? Does
he recognize this as a House of Refuge uniform?*

There was nothing I could do. I couldn't go back out
in the storm. Not tonight.

"Thank you, sir," I mumbled, swallowing hard.

"We're just glad you turned up to help," the blacksmith replied.

Then he winked and raised his voice, loud enough for
Mary to hear.

"Good thing you came to our rescue, Rocco. Knowing my daughter, she might've left me out there to freeze
while she brought the horses home."

# CHAPTER 21

*A lot of snow and a lot of lies*

"Never seen anything like it since I came over from Galway," said Mr. Hallanan the next morning, staring out the window. "Why, I doubt there ever *has* been a storm to match this in a century. And to think no one knew it was coming."

*No one,* I thought, *except Officer Reilly.*

It had started to snow the night before, after we'd brushed the horses, picked the ice from their hooves, and fed and watered them. It was already snowing hard when we tumbled into sleep. Now it was a full-on blizzard.

Outside, the world was a whirlwind of white. The snow blew sideways, driven by furious gusts that beat against the glass. Drifts would soon be up to the windowsill if this kept up. Luckily, there was a hallway leading from the family's living quarters back to the stable. After helping Mary with the chores, I hadn't had to venture out to get to the kitchen. I couldn't even imagine going outside.

"I just hope there aren't any drivers trying to take horses out in the storm," Mary said, for the third or fourth time, pacing by the window. She turned to her father and adjusted the pillow under his ankle, which he'd propped up on a chair.

"No one would be crazy enough," Mr. Hallanan assured her. "Even in New York City."

It was hard to imagine the city at a standstill. Usually morning was the busiest time. Newsboys plied their wares, shouting out the headlines. In Little Italy and the crowded neighborhood of Five Points, every corner was jammed with vegetable carts, peddlers, and women doing their shopping. Near Wall Street, men made their way to the banks, messengers delivered bags full of money, and pickpockets like Tony and Carlo started planning the day's actions.

And usually there were horses everywhere. Milk wagons began their rounds before dawn. Horses hauled crowded streetcars and omnibuses, and carts rumbled along, piled high with building supplies or produce. Little boys barely visible under the huge loads of laundry they were delivering tried to race across the streets out of the way of hooves.

None of that would happen today.

"Is your ankle any better, Da?" Mary touched it gently. It was black-and-blue with awful yellow blotches. It looked puffy and swollen.

"Hurts some," he admitted. "I don't think it's broken, though. I hope not. I don't like being laid up, not when there's work to do."

He took a sip of steaming coffee and looked over the rim of his cup at me. I could guess what he was about to ask.

"So, tell me, Rocco," he said casually, "what kind of work does your father do?"

Well, I may as well tell you now that in the next twelve minutes I told at least that many lies. I'd tried to think up a story the night before, when I lay grateful for a warm bed out of the storm. My eyes had closed before I'd gotten very far.

At least, I wasn't wearing that telltale jacket. Tim, the stableboy, kept a small stash of extra clothes in a crate by his cot. He was probably just a little taller than me, because the pants and sweater fit almost perfectly. I'd dried my House of Refuge coat in front of the small coal stove, then stuffed it under the blanket on Tim's cot.

It had been dark last night. Maybe Mr. Hallanan hadn't really recognized the House of Refuge coat. It would definitely be a good idea to keep it out of sight until I left in a day or two.

"My father's dead, two years now," I said. Lie number

one. I took a bite of the porridge Mary had made. "My mother died when I was born. After my father died, I came over from Italy to live with my uncle."

Two more lies. Three already, and that was only in answer to one question.

"I'm sorry to hear that, lad," said Mary's father. "Your English is rather good. How'd that happen, that you learned the language so quickly?"

I picked up my spoon, put it down again. This part of the story would be harder to pull off. "Well, my uncle ran a little grocery. He believed in education. So he sent me to school for a year, and I worked in the store in the afternoons."

*This sounds believable,* I thought, remembering the fellow with the sausage I'd met that first day who said he'd gone to Italian school.

I glanced out the window for more inspiration. "Then my uncle and my aunt decided to go back. He missed home—couldn't stand the cold winters here, and the snow."

Let's see, at least three more lies there, but it was getting hard to keep count. I plunged on, warming to my tale. "That was just a few weeks ago. I'll be thirteen come summer, so I decided to stay, get a place in a boardinghouse, and make my own way. I'm strong for my age. There are lots of jobs for day laborers."

At least one thing was true: I *would* be thirteen in August.

Mr. Hallanan glanced out the window and nodded. "I expect there'll be a call for Italian laborers to shovel this snow once it stops. The city will need thousands of men to dig us out. You're such a scrawny thing I wouldn't think you'd have much chance at those jobs."

He took a few more bites of porridge. I said nothing, moving my own porridge around my bowl. I'd lost my appetite.

Then, just as casually as he'd begun, he commented, "Nasty little scar on your lip, Rocco."

Behind me, where Mary was washing up in the sink, I heard a pan drop. Before I could stop myself, my hand flew to the spot. Most people outside of Little Italy didn't seem to know about the way the padroni marked the street musicians. Even the judge who sentenced me hadn't mentioned it.

Mr. Hallanan might be different. He might be the kind of man who saw a lot of what went on around him—with horses and people. The kind of man people talked to, confided in. A man who knew things and, just like Tony, had his ear to the ground.

I laughed a little. "Happened when I was a baby, at least that's what my m—papa told me."

Mr. Hallanan held my gaze and nodded. "I see. You've got to watch babies. My Mary was always getting into trouble as a babe."

"Oh, Da, you've said I was a good baby," she said quietly. Turning to me, she added, "Ma died of consumption when I was little. Da has raised me himself. I should've been a boy, though, so I could take over the blacksmith business."

Her father shook his porridge spoon at her. "None of that, Mary. I can train any man to shoe a horse. With all your schooling and your head for numbers, you'll be able to run the whole business someday. Hire your own smith and stableboys."

"That's America for you, Rocco. A poor blacksmith from an Irish village can make a name for himself, and a bright girl like Mary can get an education."

The compliment made Mary blush. I glanced around the neat kitchen, with its shiny pots and pans, and the storeroom stocked with potatoes and onions and jars of flour and oats. She kept house for her father and helped with the stable too. *Mary must be like Anna,* I thought. *Good at everything she does.*

Mr. Hallanan picked up his cup again and drained it. "Well, Rocco, I don't know what they'll be paying the men who get hired to shovel snow, probably a dollar a day. And you might prefer to do that.

"But I have a proposition for you. I can't get by without a stableboy, especially laid up with a bad ankle. I doubt Tim will be able to make it in for a few days, if this storm keeps up. Mary's good with the horses, but it's too much for one person. So how about I give you a dollar a day, plus room and board for every day you stay with us?"

Mr. Hallanan didn't ask where I had been heading

last night, or anything about the boardinghouse I'd mentioned. He didn't ask because, I thought, he had guessed the truth: I had no other place to go.

For a pickpocket like me, a dollar for a full day of work was nothing. Why, I could get that in a matter of minutes.

Still, it beat freezing in a snowdrift. The more I thought about it, the better I felt.

"Thank you, sir," I said. This time I meant it.

# CHAPTER 22

*A day to be forever known as Blizzard Monday*

$A$t first, we didn't hear it over the fierce howling wind and the incessant *rat tat tat* of snow beating against the windowpane.

Plus, Mary hadn't stopped talking. She was telling me how sad she was about Mr. Bergh being on his deathbed, and how much he had done for animals in the city.

"I'm glad we went, except of course for Da's getting hurt," she said. "Just think, those two lovely mares might have frozen to death on the street. And now you're here to help. It's amazing that you were walking by. Where were you going, anyway? You must know what to do with animals—the currycomb seemed to be part of your hand. Have you worked in a stable before?"

"Shh," Mr. Hallanan said suddenly, to my relief.

With any luck, Mary would forget what she'd asked me. "Someone's at the door. Go see to it, lad, will you?"

I ran down the hall to open the door. A round, snow-covered figure of a man stumbled inside, but not before the full force of the biting cold and blowing snow exploded into the hallway.

"Hallo there," he said, beating his arms to get more snow off. "Where's the boss? Mick, are you here?"

"Max? Are you crazy?" Mr. Hallanan called. He came into the hall from the kitchen, holding on to the wall for support. "Max Fischel! Why in heaven's name are you out in this?"

"It's a story—and I'm a reporter!" He pulled off his cap and shook snow from his curly brown hair, making a small puddle on the floor.

*A reporter?* So Max was someone who wrote the stories for newspapers. I looked at him curiously. He seemed to be in his midtwenties, with broad shoulders and twinkling dark eyes that peered out like live coals above an ice-encrusted scarf. He was almost entirely covered in snow, but that didn't seem to bother him.

"Foolish as it sounds, I really *did* start out to work this morning. How was I to know it was no ordinary snowstorm?"

"For goodness' sake, come in and get warm," urged Mary's father.

"Ah, well, that's not possible." Max's voice became serious. "Turns out I wasn't the only fool out in this nightmare. That's why I've come."

Mary reappeared with a towel. Thanking her, Max began rubbing his head with it vigorously, all the while talking a mile a minute.

"I came upon a deliveryman who'd abandoned two horses and a cart. He was almost frozen solid, poor fellow. Like me, he'd started out before he knew what he was in for," explained Max. "Told me he feared for his life if he didn't get to shelter. So he left the cart and the horses behind. It's not far, just a few blocks down on Houston and Seventh."

"I knew it!" Mary's eyes widened. "I knew there would be horses out there."

"I promised I'd find help," Max added, still rubbing his hair until it stood up like grass on top of his head. "Mary's got me so well trained I couldn't face her knowing I'd left the beasts to die. I don't know anything myself about horses or harnesses, but I came thinking Tim could be sent to bring them back."

He leaned forward a little to peer at me. "Hallo. You're not Tim. And now I see you're limping, Mick. What's happened here?"

Mary spoke first. "Last night, we had to save two mares in the freezing rain. That's when Da slipped on the ice and hurt his ankle.

"This is Rocco. He helped us. He can speak Italian *and* English," Mary went on, as though this was some great accomplishment. "The storm has kept Tim at home. Rocco and I can go get these two. He's good with animals."

"Oh, no . . . ," began Mr. Hallanan.

Mary begged, "Oh, please don't forbid me, Da. We can do it. You know it will take two—and Rocco can't do it alone."

"I wasn't going to suggest that," the blacksmith said calmly. "I can't let either of you go, Mary. And, Max, you should stay here too. You're not dressed for snow and you're already soaked through."

Now, back home, if Papa had forbidden me to do something, I would never have dared to question him. So I was surprised by what Mary did next.

She went to her father, looped her arm in his, and said softly, "Oh, Da, I know you worry. But you've raised me to be as strong as a boy. Seventh Avenue is wide—we can't get lost following it. It's no more than a few blocks—not nearly so long a trek as last night. And this time we can dress warm. It won't be like yesterday, when the storm caught us by surprise."

Mr. Hallanan's face turned red. Before he could explode, Max held up his hand. "This is my fault. Tell you what, Mick. Give me a change of clothes and I'll go with them."

Mary shot Max a grateful look, then disappeared up the stairs, taking them two at a time.

"Rocco, in the stable you'll find some extra boots and an overcoat to wear. And bring the other coat on the rack too," the blacksmith instructed. "My big coat will fit Max."

As I turned to go, I heard him tell Max, "She's

stubborn, like her mother. And she's all riled up, what with her hero, Henry Bergh, lying on his deathbed."

"Well, no doubt the Great Meddler would be proud," declared Max.

We were ready in ten minutes. I was bundled in more clothes than I'd ever had on at one time. Mary had brought me three pairs of socks, including one that came up to my knees, along with two long-sleeved shirts, a heavy wool sweater, and Tim's overcoat on top of that. I had gloves and a thick cap to pull down over my eyes. I could barely move.

Mary's father said he would ready the stable for our return.

"Da, please, go sit down. I laid everything out this morning," said Mary, reaching up to plant a kiss on his cheek. "I just knew we'd be needed for another rescue."

She used her fingers to check off all she'd done. "I put out towels to get them dry; we'll have to walk them until they get warm. I've got the currycombs ready, as well as picks to clean ice from their hooves. I put extra straw in a few empty stalls too.

"And Rocco did great last night." She smiled and tugged on her braid. "You don't have to worry, Da."

"She could run the place without me," said Mr. Hallanan with a shake of his head. He sighed. "Just be careful."

"So, you've spent time around horses, Rocco?" Max asked.

"Not horses," I told them. "Donkeys."

Mr. Hallanan gave me one more chance to back out. "I'm afraid this is more than you bargained for when you met us. Sure you're willing to go?"

"Yes, sir," I said. "I'm glad to be of help."

It was true. It had been a long time since what I did actually meant something to someone.

Back home, I'd helped Mama and Papa from the time I could walk. I fetched firewood, swept floors, shelled beans, and carried hoes and shovels down the narrow, winding streets to the fields below. I'd kept Signor Ferri's stable as clean as this. In winter, Papa trusted me to help sharpen knives and repair buckets and tools.

Everyone in Calvello worked together. I hadn't really helped anyone since coming to America. Slipping the occasional roll or crust of bread to Luigi and Marco didn't really count.

*At least, Padrone can't send them out in a storm like this,* I found myself thinking. I imagined all the street musicians huddling for warmth in the bitter cold of that dark cellar.

Mr. Hallanan insisted we take extra precautions. Mary brought rope from the stable, which her father looped around our waists, with Max in front, Mary in the middle, and me last.

When he was done, he nodded. "This way no one will get lost."

Mr. Hallanan kissed Mary and pulled open the door. We stepped out into a white, whirling nightmare. The first blast took my breath away. *We'll never get ten steps in this!*

Last night had been a battle against rain, sleet, and wind. Today was worse, the snow already so deep we plunged to our knees with every step.

As we turned the first corner, Max stopped, bringing us together in a tight circle. Overhead, ice-encrusted telegraph wires looped like an intricate, thick spiderweb. High drifts made heaps along the sidewalks; walking there was impossible.

"It might be less windy if we walk on one side of the street, away from the middle," shouted Max. We nodded and he moved into the road. The rope tightened, and we inched forward.

I tried to count my steps: "One two three, one two three." I couldn't get past three without losing my concentration.

I was amazed to realize we weren't entirely alone. Occasionally I'd look up and see a dark shape in the white blur—the lone figure of a man once, another time two people stumbling toward us, heads bent. We came across an abandoned cart, but at least this driver had taken his animals home.

A block later, we saw two dead horses, already almost buried by falling snow. Mary stopped short in front of me. But Max turned, shook his head, and pointed down the street. We weren't there yet. When we did reach the horses, we found them still in harness, miserable, helpless, their heads bowed. Max fumbled with the rope to untie us so we could get to work. Mary stepped forward, pulling on my arm to follow her.

She approached the first horse and grabbed the bridle. He seemed too numb to move and didn't shy away from her. It took a long time to unhitch the pair, but Mary didn't stop, though her movements were slow.

Just as she handed the reins of one of the horses to me, I saw a figure out of the corner of my eye. I pointed and mouthed, "Look!"

Max followed my gaze. A boy was stumbling toward us, his arms flailing as he tried to plow through the snow. All at once he tripped, plunging into a drift. His face and almost his entire head disappeared.

"I'll get him!" Max pushed through the snow, reached under the boy's arms, and pulled him up.

He could not have been more than ten. He wore no hat or muffler; his face was red and shiny, as though covered by a thin sheet of ice. His whole body shook with sobs. He struggled to talk.

I managed to make out one word: "job." He must have been on his way to work, afraid he would lose whatever job he had—probably sweeping a factory floor—if he didn't show up.

After talking to the boy for a few minutes, Max trudged back and put his mouth to my ear. "He doesn't live far. But it's in the opposite direction from Barrow Street," he said. "He can't make it alone. I don't dare let him go by himself."

I shouted, "Take the rope. It might help him walk."

Mary had finished with the other horse by now. Max used his hands to tell her what he planned to do. She nodded, pointing to me and at herself, then up Seventh Avenue, the way we'd come. It was hard to talk— the wind snatched the words from our mouths before they were out. But we understood. Mary and I would go home alone.

It didn't seem to matter what direction we headed; the wind and snow came at us, battering, hammering, pounding us with furious, unrelenting gusts and shards of sharp, icy flakes.

Snow had already half filled the footsteps we'd left on our way down the street, but we could still make them out enough to follow the trail. Sometimes having the body of the horse on one side of me gave a little protection. Mostly, I had to pull and coax the exhausted beast along behind me. In the deepest drifts, Mary and I took turns trudging ahead to break a path for the animals.

"I don't want them to trip," she yelled into my ear once. "We can't let them go down."

I nodded. Breathing was hard, talking harder. We had to go *so* slow. Time stopped. I wasn't as cold and wet as yesterday, but I felt the storm pummeling and thrashing me, sucking every drop of energy and warmth out of my body. Soon I would be emptied out. Yesterday I'd been rowing across the Harlem River. Now I was following Meddlin' Mary through deep snow. How had the weather—how had everything—changed so quickly?

Once, I tripped, pulling down so hard on the reins I was afraid the horse would go down too. Luckily, he stood steady. I stopped to catch my breath, hiding my face against his neck. His mane was crusted hard with ice.

"Good boy," I told him. "*Amore mio*. You are a sweetheart. You won't turn on me like Old Biter."

The street signs were mostly unreadable. After what seemed like hours, I looked up to see an *L* above me. I squinted and made out more letters: LEROY STREET. Were we close? At least Mary knew her way.

A little while on, she waved her arm. Barrow Street. We had made it.

Mary's father was waiting. Despite his sprained ankle, he'd cleared a narrow path from the street into the courtyard beyond the archway. He had also moved enough snow so we could open the stable door.

Inside, the blacksmith took Mary's horse from her, ordering her into the kitchen to change by the warm stove. Hobbling as best he could, he began brushing the worst of the snow from the animal's legs.

I'd been trying to do the same, but I couldn't seem to get my body to do what my brain wanted. After a few minutes, the blacksmith grabbed my arm. He had tied the first horse and was holding out his hand to take the reins of mine.

"Go get warm. I've got him," he ordered. "I've put dry clothes by the stove in the kitchen. And there's a pot of coffee. Drink a cup and change. Then come back fast as you can."

I did as he said, passing Mary on her way back, her hair in wild, loose curls, her cheeks raw and flaming. I could barely make my fingers work to undo the buttons on my shirt. My toes began to sting with pain as the warmth seeped through my socks.

I was back in ten minutes. Mr. Hallanan was rubbing down the horse I'd led back, while Mary tended to the other. The horses looked miserable, their sides heaving. We worked on both animals for an hour or more, rubbing them with a currycomb, picking ice out of their hooves, walking them up and down.

Every so often, the blacksmith would stop to feel their ears. "A horse's ears shouldn't be too cold or too hot. They're getting back to normal."

Eventually we gave them some water and led them to the stalls Mary had made ready with fresh bedding. Mine whinnied softly and pushed his nose into my shoulder as if to thank me.

As we set out the towels to dry near the potbellied stove in the stable, Mary told her father, "It wasn't Max's fault he couldn't come back with us. He couldn't let that boy die."

Mr. Hallanan had been angry when we returned

alone. Now he sighed. "I understand. But this is the last time. We can't save every horse in the city. I fear beasts and people both will lose their lives in this storm. It's gotten worse every minute since you went out, and shows no sign of letting up."

"We did well, though, didn't we?" Mary said happily, her cheeks still red.

"Your mother would have been proud, darling." Her father reached out and smoothed Mary's flyaway curls.

We were still for a moment. I thought about Mama, and my thoughts spilled out into words.

"You were as strong as my mother, Mary," I exclaimed without thinking, just the way Mama had always warned me about. "She used to carry heavy loads of firewood up the mountain, loads almost as heavy as ones a man could shoulder. Uh . . . well, I mean, that's what my father said, anyway."

Mr. Hallanan flashed me a look but said nothing. I'd almost forgotten I'd said my mother died in childbirth.

That's the trouble with lies. Sometimes it's hard to keep them straight.

# CHAPTER 23

*A short and slightly sentimental chapter
introducing a horse*

One fall, when Anna and I were in the forest gathering firewood, we found a small bird. I couldn't say what kind it was, and Mama didn't recognize it either. She supposed it must have been blown off course by a storm. The little stranger lay on the ground, feathers ruffled, heart racing. Anna made soft noises, then cupped it in her hands and put it in the hollow of a tree.

We never knew if the bird made it. But we were glad that at least it had a chance to rest peacefully. I felt much like that creature the rest of Blizzard Monday. I too had been blown off track, to some new and unfamiliar place. Still, for that afternoon, gazing out the window at the fierce and raging blizzard, I was safe. I didn't have to scheme and plan about what to do next. I could just rest, dry and warm.

Oh, we did move some, of course. All twelve stalls were full, so Mary and I had a lot of work to do. We checked on the horses often, especially the four we called the "storm horses." All seemed well; they greeted us with gentle, contented whinnies and low, breathy, nickering snuffles.

"They're as happy to be inside as we are," said Mary. "Aren't you glad we rescued them, Rocco? I'm going to write our whole adventure down in my journal."

Mary Hallanan, it seemed, was a girl who loved stories.

"I wasn't scared even once," she went on as we walked through the hall that led from the stable to the kitchen.

"Not once?" I teased. She reminded me so much of Anna, who would never admit to being frightened of anything.

"Well, yes, I was a *little* scared last night, especially when Da fell. Not today, though. I like walking in snow better than on ice."

Later she made a stew with beef, potatoes, onions, and carrots. Mr. Hallanan worked on polishing tack. I offered to help; he showed me how he liked it done, explaining how the various harnesses, bits, and bridles worked for different kinds of carts. As I cleaned and oiled a leather bridle, I was filled with a sense of comfort I couldn't place at first. It was the feeling of being home.

The blacksmith's house was much grander than the two small rooms in Calvello where I'd grown up. Yet I didn't feel too out of place. Maybe, I realized, because it was the only time since coming to America that I'd actually seen or been with a family. I suddenly missed my own family more than ever. Tears stung my eyes. I bit my lip, lowered my head, and cleared my throat.

"You all right there, Rocco?" asked the blacksmith, shooting me one of his keen glances.

I nodded wordlessly. It was too confusing to think about my family—how much I had disappointed Papa and Mama, my promise to Anna, what I could have done differently. It was confusing to think about a lot of things.

Only one thought cheered me up: The city would be so busy shoveling out from the snow that one runaway from the House of Refuge might soon be forgotten.


"Tell you what I'd like, Mary darling," the blacksmith said a while later, not taking his eyes off the soft leather he was oiling. "Why don't you read to us from your favorite book? You might start at the beginning. I don't expect Rocco's ever heard it."

"Do you know *Black Beauty*?" Mary asked.

I shook my head. I turned back to my work when she went to fetch the book, not able to look Mr. Hallanan in the eye. We sat in silence. The lies I had told him seemed to be piled up on the table between us, as solid as the objects we held in our hands.

Mary was back in a minute, holding up a well-worn volume for me to see. "It's called *Black Beauty: The Autobiography of a Horse,* by Anna Sewell. It's the only book she ever wrote."

"Autobiography?" I queried, repeating the unfamiliar word.

"Autobiographies are stories people tell of their own lives. This one is Beauty's story, as if he could write and talk," she explained. "Of course, it's just made-up."

*Autobiography.* This was almost as astonishing as the snow outside. Someone—this person named Anna Sewell—had believed the story of a horse's life was worth telling.

Mary opened the book and held up the title page. "*Black Beauty* was published in London in 1877, about ten years ago. It begins with Beauty telling about his earliest memories."

Her father gave her an encouraging nod. "Go on, lass, I don't tire of this story."

Mary began, reading the words as if she knew them by heart:

"*The first place that I can well remember was a large pleasant meadow with a pond of clear water in it. Some shady trees leaned over it, and rushes and water-lilies grew at the deep end. Over the hedge on one side we looked into a plowed field, and on the other we looked over a gate at our master's house, which stood by the roadside; at the top of the meadow was a* grove of fir trees, and at the bottom a running brook overhung by a steep bank.

"While I was young I lived upon my mother's milk, as I could not eat grass. In the daytime I ran by her side, and at night I lay down close by her. When it was hot we used to stand by the pond in the shade of the trees, and when it was cold we had a nice warm shed near the grove...."

There was more. But after a while, though I wanted to keep listening, my head drooped on the table, and the bridle slipped from my fingers. The next thing I knew, the blacksmith was shaking me, urging me to take myself off to sleep in the stable.

# CHAPTER 24

*An interlude with horses;*
*Mary imparts a lesson in meddling*

When I woke up Tuesday morning, I was sure the savage storm would be over. It wasn't.

We didn't have much time to sit around and read *Black Beauty,* though. Before breakfast, Mr. Hallanan handed me a shovel and showed me what he wanted done. "If we don't make a start on it now, we'll never get out. Try to make a path from the street to the courtyard. The hardest part will be finding a place to pile the snow up."

After two hours, Mary banged on the window and motioned me in. I looked behind me. You could barely see any dent in the deep white covering. I'd have to do more later; it would take ages to make a path wide enough for a cart.

Mr. Hallanan's ankle was a little better, so he spent

most of the day "puttering," as he called it, in the stable and the blacksmith shop—moving tools around, cleaning, sorting nails and horseshoes into their correct trays (though it all looked perfectly neat and tidy to me).

After shoveling, I worked in the stable with Mary. We mucked out stalls, fed and watered the horses, and gave each one a thorough brushing with the currycomb. Curious heads poked out of stall doors, and dark, liquid eyes followed our movements. I liked the smells of hay, oiled leather, and horse sweat. I didn't even mind mucking out manure.

These animals were patient creatures, at least compared to Old Biter, who kicked his stall door if I took too long to bring the hay. Of course, he wouldn't be having that problem now: That sailor was probably feeding him plates piled with mountains of spaghetti.

Mr. Hallanan hobbled in to check the condition of the four storm horses. He had us walk them back and forth so he could be sure they weren't lame. Next he ran a practiced hand carefully over each, searching for signs of sores or ill treatment. The blacksmith brought Mary's attention to the cart horse she'd led in the first night.

"This mare is a bit underweight, I'd say. Give her some extra hay for now," he instructed before leaving us to finish our work. "When the driver shows up, I'll make him a deal on boarding them here he won't be able to refuse. That way, we'll be able to keep an eye on her.

"I suppose I'm a meddler in my own way," he chuckled.

"The horses like you. I think you're a good stablegirl," I told Mary. I'd been thinking that as I watched her sure, unhurried movements.

She laughed. "I should be—I grew up in here. Da tells me that when I was little, I would cry unless he let me help with the horses. So he would sit me up on a stool so I could brush them. Only the old, gentle ones, of course. My mother called me the Stable Princess."

"Do you remember much about her?"

"Just a little. She got consumption and died when I was four. Da says she helped make their dreams come true. They got married in Ireland and came here when she was only sixteen. She went to work in a factory to help Da start the business.

"We think about her every day. I'm sorry about your mother, Rocco," Mary added in a soft voice. "You must wish you had even one memory of her."

"It . . . it's all right." I was glad to bend over a broom so she couldn't see my red face.

Mary told me that her father had worked for someone else for several years, until her parents had earned enough to rent a small shop here on Barrow Street. Eventually he bought the house and the one next to it, turning it into the shop and stable he owned today.

"Are all these horses yours?"

"Oh, no! Only Sheridan, the old gelding in the back," she said. "He was so broken down he was left for dead on the street, but my father nursed him back to health. The other horses board here; most are owned by cab or cart drivers.

"Da comes from a long line of blacksmiths in Ireland. He knows as much about horses as anyone in the city," she told me proudly as she filled a bucket with water from a tap near the stable door. Once Mary got started talking, you didn't have to say much to keep her going.

"That's how we got to know Henry Bergh."

I thought about that first day, when I'd seen Mr. Bergh and Mary in action. I bit my tongue. Telling her that now would raise too many questions.

"Mr. Bergh came to Da a few years ago to ask his advice about the design for the first horse ambulance for the society he founded—the American Society for the Prevention of Cruelty to Animals," Mary went on.

"An ambulance?"

"A vehicle that transports injured horses off the streets so they can be cared for properly," Mary explained, carrying her bucket to replenish the water trough in one of the stalls. "I remember that day Mr. Bergh came to visit. I was only eight. I'd just finished reading *Black Beauty,* and then here was a man who cared about helping horses as much as I did. And he was doing it!"

I could imagine Mary peppering Mr. Bergh with questions. Mary was inside a stall now. I couldn't see her face but she kept talking.

"I love *Black Beauty,* but it's just a story, of course.

What matters is . . . I don't know . . . what you do once the story is inside you.

"In real life, horses don't have voices." Mary emerged, latching the stall door behind her and reaching up to stroke the nose of the horse inside. "*We* have to be their voices."

"What do you mean?"

"When we see cruel or unfair treatment, we have to speak up, because horses can't do it for themselves. It's not easy for me to stand up to strangers and ask them to get off a crowded bus or streetcar," she admitted. "But Mr. Bergh always says that to make things change, you need a strong heart."

I stared down at the floor, the image of Luigi and Marco struggling to push their harp along the cobblestones clear in my mind. Street musicians didn't have voices either.

And what about Signor Ferri? What if I had been brave enough to really stand up to him?

"It doesn't seem like one person can do much, though," I murmured.

"You're wrong, Rocco." Mary looked right at me then, her brown eyes keen. "Think about it. Anna Sewell was one person. Mr. Bergh is just one person. But he started a whole society of people to help make things better, people who will carry on this work."

"He's rich, though."

"You're not rich, and you changed something," she

declared. "We both did. We saved those horses. And if we hadn't been on that street yesterday, that boy Max took home might've died. We might not write a book or start a society, but we can do something. At least, we can try."

I didn't answer. I didn't know what to say. I wasn't much like Mary. I wasn't brave, and I certainly didn't have a strong heart. I was a liar, a bandit.

As for the one time I *had* meddled—that night in Signor Ferri's stable (which, I promise, I will give an account of quite soon)—well, that had only made me a castaway.

I wondered what Mary Hallanan would do if she knew the truth about me.

# BOOK FOUR

## *The Battle in Bandits' Roost*

With appetite ground to keenest edge by a hunger that is never fed, the children of the poor grow up in joyless homes to lives of wearisome toil that claims them at an age when the play of their happier fellows has but just begun. Has a yard of turf been laid and a vine been coaxed to grow within their reach, they are banished and barred out from it as from a heaven that is not for such as they.

I came upon a couple of youngsters in a Mulberry Street yard a while ago that were chalking on the fence their first lesson in "writin'." And this is what they wrote: "Keeb of te Grass." They had it by heart, for there was not, I verily believe, a green sod within a quarter of a mile. Home to them is an empty name. Pleasure? A gentleman once catechized a ragged class in a down-town public school on this point, and recorded the result: Out of forty-eight boys twenty had never seen the Brooklyn Bridge that was scarcely five minutes' walk away, three only had been in Central Park, fifteen had known the joy of a ride in a horse-car.

The street, with its ash-barrels and its dirt, the river that runs foul with mud, are their domain.

—JACOB RIIS, *How the Other Half Lives*

# CHAPTER 25

*I meet other meddlers and make a speech*

On Wednesday morning, the city began digging out. I was up at five to do more shoveling. Later the skies cleared and the sun came out. Spring had decided to return. The snow would melt eventually, but not right away—there was simply too much of it.

By noon, the stable was a bustling place. I didn't stop for hours. Mr. Hallanan sent me running here and there, fetching bridles and bringing horses. A few of their owners had gotten jobs hauling snow. And since the men stored their vehicles along with their animals, we had to dig wagons and carts out of the drifts too.

The owner of the underweight mare appeared. "Board your team here from now on. You owe me that much, my friend," I heard Mick Hallanan say. "I've got an ankle the size of a tree trunk because of you. I'll give you a bargain on hay. And just look at your mare, her coat's as shiny as the Hudson River in moonlight, thanks to my new stableboy here.

"You'll cut a fine figure on the streets with this pair," he told the man. "Times are changing. These days, people like to see a driver who takes pride in his team. It's good for business."

Mr. Hallanan winked at me. The deal was done.

"Is it always so busy?" I asked Mary breathlessly as I trotted by to grab a harness.

She nodded, blowing some straggling curls out of her eyes as she lugged a bucket of water. Mary wouldn't be able to get through the snowy streets to school for a few days yet. "It's like this early in the morning, before I leave for school. Tim finishes up and Da gets busy shoeing horses. I'm back in the evening to help when the boarders come back in."

We were so busy that it was late afternoon before I finally had time to brush Mr. Hallanan's horse, Sheridan. Mary said he was named after a famous Civil War cavalry general her father admired. He was my favorite. He looked wise, and his scars reminded me of the horses in *Black Beauty*. If he could talk, Sheridan would have stories to tell about the past.

"*Ti voglio bene.*" I whispered the familiar words of love as I brushed his coat. He twitched one ear back and nickered softly. I chuckled. "So, you like Italian, do you?"

Suddenly the quiet was interrupted by the noise of angry boots.

"Who are you?" came a voice I didn't know.

I turned. This boy with the brash blue eyes and square chin must be Tim. I decided to tease him a little.

"Hallo, Tim. Finally come back, have you?" I asked pleasantly. "Now, if I had a good job like this, I wouldn't be slacking off on account of a little snow."

I watched him tighten his hands into fists by his side. Then I grinned. "Don't worry, I'm not after your place; I'll soon be gone. I think you'll find Mr. Hallanan in the kitchen. He twisted his ankle but it's getting better. He'll be glad to have you back."

As he stomped off, I called after him, "Tim, I appreciate the loan of your clothes."

That was truer than he could know.

As it turned out, Tim wouldn't be back to work right away. Tim's father delivered milk; when he'd tried to do his usual rounds on Blizzard Monday, he'd fallen, breaking his right arm. So Tim would be needed every morning for the next few weeks to help his father drive the milk wagon and climb in and out to put bottles on doorsteps.

"Tim will come when he can to help in the smithy," Mr. Hallanan told me later. "I'll be shorthanded, though, especially once Mary goes back to school. So I have a proposition for you, Rocco. What would you think about staying on for a while longer to help in the stable? Same terms as before—a dollar a day.

"So far I've been pleased. You've done well." He looked me straight in the eye. "I'll continue to expect an honest day's work. Can you do that?"

I felt sure Mr. Hallanan suspected I was a runaway. Yet he was still willing to give me a chance. I made myself meet his eyes. "I can, sir. You have my word."

He held my gaze for a long moment. "I'll hold you to that promise, lad."

"I like working with the horses," I told him. "They're nicer than some donkeys."

And that was true. I liked the feel of their soft, silky noses when they pushed their heads at me, looking for an apple or a lump of sugar. I liked the noises they made as they shifted in their stalls or peered out to see what I was doing while I swept the floor.

Being a blacksmith, Mr. Hallanan knew as much about horses' hooves as Pug or Tony did about pickpocketing. Mary's father hadn't forgotten his resolve during the storm either. He'd been using the evenings to perfect the design for his new invention: a rubber hoof pad for horses—the same rubber shoe he'd been rambling about the night we met.

He tried to explain the problems he'd had with earlier versions. "We want something made of leather and rubber so the horse won't slip. I think I'm getting close to coming up with a good design."

As I looked at the table strewn with his sketches, I could see the determination that had made his dreams come true. Mary took after both her parents.

On Wednesday evening, Max Fischel showed up as we were sitting down to eat. "Ah, just in time for Mary's famous stew," he said with an elfish grin. "Not that I planned it that way."

Max had come to return the rope, along with Mr. Hallanan's coat. He also brought sad news. "We got word at the newspaper that Henry Bergh died Monday morning. The Great Meddler is gone."

"A good man," said the blacksmith, putting a hand on Mary's arm. Her eyes glistened with tears.

Bowls of stew sat before us, but no one was eating. I started to spear a carrot with my fork, then put it down again.

"His work will go on." Max looked at Mary as he spoke. "Not just with animal rights. You may remember the case of that little girl called Mary Ellen. Henry Bergh and his friends stepped in to save her, and then they started a society to prevent cruelty to children."

His words surprised me. So Mr. Bergh *had* been concerned about people too. If there was a society to prevent cruelty to children, why didn't people in it close down Padrone's den? I thought I knew the answer already: No one really knew the stories of boys like me, Luigi, Marco, and Giuseppe. No one noticed us on the street or saw inside 45 Crosby Street. The street musicians might as well be ghosts.

"Mr. Bergh lived a worthy life," Mr. Hallanan was saying.

"I know." Mary lifted her chin. "I'm not stopping just because he's gone, Da. I want to keep inspecting streets and writing letters to the city to make sure dangerous spots get fixed."

"I never thought you would stop, darling girl."

Max picked up his fork and began attacking his stew. "All I can say is, I can't keep up with you, Mary. Or Jacob Riis either. Most nights, after chasing stories all day, I'm home with my feet by the stove, while Jacob's just getting started."

Finally! We could eat. Shoveling had made me hungry. I chewed for a while. Mary's stew, I thought, might be even more delicious than sausages. Then I heard my name.

"That reminds me, Mick. I wonder if you can spare Rocco tomorrow night," Max was saying. "Jacob wants to get back out taking photographs in the evenings. It seems being cooped up in the storm gave him a new idea. He thinks the lectures he's been giving aren't enough—now he wants to write a book and put pictures in it."

"Who's Jacob Riis?" I mumbled in between bites.

"A newspaperman like me," said Max. "A few months ago, he heard that the Germans have invented a contraption to make flash photography possible. Since then, he's been on a crusade. He bought a camera and has been taking pictures to tell the story of the tenements and the people of the Lower East Side.

"Jacob is struck by the notion that one half of the world doesn't know how the other half lives. He's convinced that if only people could *see* the conditions in the tenements, things would change. He's convinced that photographs are the answer.

"I'm his eyes and ears in the Jewish quarters," Max went on, turning to me. "Rocco, after Mary mentioned the other day that you spoke Italian, I got to thinking. You could smooth the way for Mr. Riis with Italian immigrants, just like I do with Jewish families."

"What would I do?"

"It's not hard. I help translate, carry his equipment, that sort of thing," Max replied. "I suggested to him that you could be his guide when he visits places like Mulberry Bend, that desperately poor section of Mulberry Street, and Bandits' Roost."

*Mulberry Street and Bandits' Roost—the very places I don't want to get anywhere near!*

"It's fine with me," agreed Mary's father. "Rocco will be taking Tim's place for a few weeks. He should be able to do both jobs."

Mr. Hallanan turned to look at me, and maybe I imagined the challenge in his eyes. "What do you say, Rocco? Is that all right with you?"

I tried not to squirm. But I couldn't think of a way out. Then Mary leaned forward to give me a little smile of encouragment.

"Yes, it's fine," I managed to stammer out. "I would love to help Mr. Riis if I can."

And that's how I ended up agreeing to meet Jacob Riis at the Mulberry Street police station at eight the next evening.

Just the idea of being anywhere near a police station—especially one that I had been inside of as a convicted pickpocket—was enough to make my stomach churn. Would the House of Refuge have sent out my description? Would some copper take one look at me and put me in handcuffs then and there?

Nevertheless, the next night, I made my way to the police station at 301 Mulberry Street. I wore a sweater and pulled my cap down low on my forehead. I left my gray jacket hidden under Tim's blanket. Mary's father hadn't mentioned it. Maybe I'd just imagined he'd recognized it that night. Maybe all he'd been thinking about had been the pain in his ankle and getting those horses rescued.

*When I leave my job as a stableboy, I won't take that jacket with me,* I decided. *I'll bunch it up at the bottom of the crate where Tim keeps his clothes. Or maybe I'll even dump it in the river!*

It was about a mile walk, though it took longer than usual, with the piles of snow still clogging every street and sidewalk. Soon the neighborhoods began to look more familiar. I was getting close to 45 Crosby Street, which was only a few blocks from the station. I hadn't been back since I'd been arrested.

I wondered about Luigi, Marco, Giuseppe, and the other boys. Were they out on the streets again? Had the padrone fed them during the storm? Before leaving Barrow Street, I'd eaten a full bowl of Mary's stew. Between Tony's mob and the regular food at the House of Refuge, I'd almost forgotten the hunger of those first weeks in America. Luigi and Marco had been hungry every day for a long time now—that is, if they were still alive.

Outside the police station, I spotted a copper chatting with a trim man wearing oval wire-framed glasses and an intense frown of concentration. The man was balancing a camera and a long pole-like apparatus. *This must be Jacob Riis,* I thought. I stood a little ways off, hoping to be noticed, and was relieved when he spoke to me first.

"Oh, are you Max's young friend?" he asked. Then Mr. Riis said goodbye to the copper, who didn't give me a second glance. "Time for work. My new assistant is here."

"I'm Rocco."

"And I'm Jacob. Let's go, then," he said, handing me the pole. "I want to get shots of the police-station lodging on Elizabeth Street. It houses Italian women most nights."

He walked so quickly I had to skip to keep up. "What exactly will I do, sir?"

"Ah, well, it's not easy for a stranger to barge in and take pictures, especially since I don't speak the language," he said, not slowing his pace. "I'd like you to explain my purpose to the lodgers gathered here, and tell them what will happen when the flash gun goes off.

And I might sometimes ask you to translate when I do interviews."

"Max told me a little bit about what you do."

"Good. Well, as he probably mentioned, I want to show the true state of the tenements," he told me. "I've been writing stories, but that doesn't seem enough. Flash photography allows me to light up dark places—to bring the lives of these people into the light so they can be seen."

"I don't think most people want to see," I found myself saying. Then I wondered if I'd said too much.

He slowed and looked at me closely for the first time. "What makes you say that?"

"I guess I think it's easy to pass poor people by, to walk by the tenement houses."

"You're right. That's my challenge: to make images so powerful that more people will stop, will finally see—especially people with the power to change things.

"Mulberry Bend is such a maze of alleys and grim, dirty rooms." Mr. Riis gestured at the wooden tenements on every side. He spoke in a low, intense voice, almost as if he was talking to himself. I had to step closer to catch his words. "Sometimes I just can't bear to see the children here. They have so little. And their poor mothers struggle to feed them. I feel . . . I feel called to bear witness to it, perhaps because I'm an immigrant myself. And if I can capture all this in a book for people who never come here, I feel sure it can create ripples of change."

*A book.* Maybe Mr. Riis was right. After all, *Black Beauty* had changed Mary's life.

"Some of these tenements aren't fit for human beings and should be torn down," Mr. Riis went on, shaking his head. He adjusted the camera strap on his shoulder and kept walking. "Decent housing is possible. We need to make laws so landlords provide clean water and safe buildings. We need to prosecute them if they don't."

He sighed. "I just need people to see." Then he shot a glance at my face. "I'm sorry, Rocco. I expect I've overwhelmed you. I've been giving so many lectures these days that my dear wife tells me I'm in danger of making a speech whenever I open my mouth.

"Just last night, she complained I was addressing the children at the table as if I was speaking to an audience. And all I wanted was for someone to pass the butter."

Inside the Elizabeth Street station, Mr. Riis spoke to one of the police officers and then led the way along a dim hallway. He stopped before a wooden door.

"This is it. The police have set aside these rooms so people don't have to sleep on the streets." He began to fiddle with his equipment. "As I mentioned, this lodging room is used by Italian women, so you can explain to them in Italian what will happen. Then I'll take one or two photographs."

I swallowed hard, staring at the closed door in front of me. I might have spurted out random thoughts, but

I'd certainly never made a speech before. I watched as Mr. Riis unfolded a tripod, placed the camera on it, and loaded a glass plate into a special drawer in the camera. The camera had a cord attached too.

He chuckled. "Don't look so bewildered, Rocco. It's quite easy. I'll even show you, if you like. We simply press this button on the cord to take the picture once the flash lights up the room.

"Now for the flash powder. I use a special chemical mixture developed by my friend Henry Piffard from the Amateur Photographers' Club, where I learned to take pictures. Works brilliantly." What he had called the flash gun actually looked like a broom handle with a narrow rectangular tray on top. Mr. Riis poured the chemicals into the tray.

"Lighting this powder causes a small chemical explosion and a flash of light. I time the exposure to the light, which allows me to take pictures at night and inside. Since the light and noise of the flash gun can be startling, please tell everyone not to be frightened."

When he was ready, I opened the door. Six or seven women were huddled around a potbellied stove. Their skirts and faces were smudged with dirt. The brick walls were lined with soot. The floor was cold, bare stone.

The women looked tired, their heads bowed. They reminded me of the horses Mary and I had rescued, who had stood waiting patiently in the snow, enduring the storm because they had no other choice.

I stepped forward.

"*Buona sera.* Good evening," I began. I kept on in Italian. "This gentleman is Signor Jacob Riis. He is a good man who cares about people. He has come to take a picture so that others may see the hardships you suffer."

I took a ragged breath. *What would Mary say now?* I wondered.

One woman raised her head, staring straight at me. She had a strong, bold face and piercing eyes. Her clothes were ragged, but I could see she wasn't ashamed. "Always be proud of who you are," Mama had told us.

I muddled on. "I know you have strong hearts. Mr. Riis does too. But he has a strong voice too: People listen to his words. They look at his pictures.

"Signor Riis will take a photograph now. A photograph shows a moment in time. It lasts forever, like a fresco in a church back home. First will come a noise. *Whoosh!* Then there will be a sudden bright light. But don't worry, you will be safe."

The match was lit, the powder exploded, and the room burst into light.


"You did well, Rocco," said Mr. Riis. "Thank you. I'll show you the picture in a few days, once I develop it in my darkroom."

I felt relieved to have gotten through that first speech. Our work wasn't over for the night, though. We spent the next two hours poking into alleyways and visiting other police-station lodging rooms. I made more speeches, watching closely as Mr. Riis took his photographs.

The night air was growing cold when Mr. Riis stopped and pointed. "Look—those three boys are sleeping around that metal grate. Probably it's a steam vent, so there might be a little warm air coming out.

"I have a son about that age," he murmured.

He proceeded to set up his tripod, fix the camera on top of it, and once again pour powder into the flash-gun tray.

He handed a small box of matches to me and whispered, "You do it, but be careful. Make sure to hold the powder tray away from your face. Don't want your eyebrows singed off."

*Whoosh!*

The boys were so tired they didn't even wake.

# CHAPTER 26

*Containing matters of much significance relating
to a locket, a dog, and a most difficult reunion*

Now, you may be thinking that my path had become quite smooth. Thanks to Mary and her father, I might even be on my way to becoming a reformed and useful member of society.

Maybe you're guessing that Mary's father would give me a permanent job. I would send money home to my family, live peacefully with meddlers, and give up moll-buzzing and other nefarious pursuits. I would escape the snares of the House of Refuge, my padrone, and my old pickpocketing mob.

Well, if that's what you're thinking, you're wrong.

Oh, I suppose it might have turned out that way. But late one spring afternoon, Mr. Riis sent for me, and everything that had been going right began to go wrong again.

By now I had been helping Mr. Riis for a couple of weeks. I'd made more speeches, and he'd been teaching me how to use his camera. He'd even let me try a few photographs on my own.

I still kept a wary eye out for coppers and my padrone when venturing out alone, but didn't worry so much when I was with Mr. Riis. No one suspected me of being a runaway or a street musician when I was with him. People saw me as Mr. Riis's bright, neatly dressed young assistant. Police officers gave me a friendly nod or smile.

Mr. Riis was more serious than Max, and often we walked through the tenement neighborhoods without saying a word, though his keen eyes took in everything around us. Probably, I thought, he was thinking about what he would put in his book.

But, on this particular afternoon, as we left our meeting spot by the Mulberry Street police station, he suddenly began to tell me a story.

"I had a dog die for me outside a station like this years ago," he began.

Instantly I remembered Saint Rocco, who, to be honest, I hadn't thought about (or prayed to) for a long time. Now I recalled how a dog had befriended him. Adjusting the flash gun on my shoulder, I looked up at Mr. Riis. "What happened, sir?"

"I arrived from Denmark when I was twenty-one. I traveled around doing odd jobs for a while, but eventually, like so many others, I found myself in this neighborhood, as homeless and dirty and grimy as everyone else," he told me. "Sometimes I thought of ending my life.

"One night, an abandoned dog attached himself to me. I believe that had it not been for the comfort of another breathing creature next to me, I might have thrown myself in the river, my despair was so great."

The crowds around us were thick, and Mr. Riis stepped into a doorway to continue his story. "I got a bed in a police-station lodging on Church Street, much like the one on Elizabeth Street where we took the photograph of the women.

"I had a gold locket with me, which held a lock of my future wife's hair. I fell asleep, and when I woke up, it was gone. Someone had stolen my most precious—my only—possession. That just about broke my heart."

*A locket* ... My thoughts whirred. The locket I'd grabbed probably meant a lot to that young woman too. Maybe it had a picture of her sweetheart, or even of her dead mother, inside. No wonder she had screamed.

"When I complained it was missing, the police officer didn't believe someone like me could have owned anything valuable," Mr. Riis went on. "He told the doorman to kick me out. But outside, as the man was shoving me down the steps, my four-footed friend tried to come to my aid."

He took a breath and paused, almost as if he didn't want to say what happened next. "The man picked up my dog and threw him to the curb, smashing his head and killing him. I was stunned. Then a blind rage rose inside me, like a building bursting into flame. I began to scream and pelt the police station with rocks or anything I could grab from the street."

"They must have locked you up!"

"No, but they got rid of me another way. They put me on a ferry to New Jersey and told me not to come back," he said with a wry smile. "From there, I continued my wandering ways, picking up work where I could. I already knew English, and decided I wanted to become a newspaperman. Eventually I came back and got a job as a reporter.

"But I will tell you this, Rocco. Now I am back. And I haven't forgotten that night at the Church Street station," Mr. Riis said. "I haven't forgotten the outrage I felt, or the men and women I met who, like me, were just doing their best to survive.

"That's why I do this. It could be me. It *was* me."

We kept walking, both of us lost in thought. Mr. Riis, I felt sure, was remembering his dog. I was thinking of Signor Ancarola's silver blade. Then Mr. Riis said, "Ah, here we are. Bandits' Roost."

I stopped in my tracks. I'd been so caught up in the story I hadn't realized where we were heading. It was too late to protest. Pulling my cap low, I trailed behind Mr. Riis. In the alleyway, several young men and teenage boys stood idly chatting.

At our approach, everyone stopped talking. Mr. Riis nodded at me to begin. I'd made the speech a number of times by now, but never like this. Never in front of anyone I knew.

For I'd spotted Tony right away. He didn't acknowledge me, though I saw his eyebrows lift in surprise. He looked dapper as usual, with a new bowler hat, a vest, and a jacket with a gold watch on a chain. *No doubt lifted from a sucker,* I thought.

I took a ragged breath. "Excuse me. This man with me is Signor Jacob Riis, who humbly begs your pardon for the interruption. He is here to take a picture."

"Speak up, boy. We can't hear you back here," called a voice. "Did you say that stranger's come to pass out dollar bills with pictures on them?"

Tony and the other thieves snickered. I flushed and shuffled my feet. Could I go through with this?

I spied Carlo, his elbow perched on a wooden staircase. He cocked his head at me but didn't say a word.

"I know many of you have families to support. I know you are good sons who came here with dreams," I went on, my voice louder now.

I turned, pointing at Jacob Riis. "Mr. Riis is an immigrant like us. He has slept in police-station lodgings. He has been homeless and without a job. Now he tells stories and takes photographs to make things better in our neighborhood, so your families can drink clean water, and so landlords will build better houses."

Jacob Riis had finished setting up his camera. He gave me a quick nod.

"There will be a noise and a flash of light," I announced.

We would not know it until much, much later, but the photograph Jacob Riis took that day would become one of his most famous pictures of all.


"Rocco, we meet again."

I wasn't surprised to hear Tony's voice in my ear or to feel his touch on my elbow. I'd suspected Mr. Riis and I were being followed all the way to the office across from the Mulberry Street station that he and Max Fischel shared with other police reporters.

After Mr. Riis had thanked me and stepped inside, I didn't have long to wait. Now I found myself being steered back into the crowds of Mulberry Bend, back toward Bandits' Roost.

Carlo was already there, and he spouted his usual cheerful greeting. "Hallo, Rocco. Where've you been all these months? We heard you were on a certain *island*."

At first, I thought they might leave me alone. Then Tony leaned over me, pushing me against the wall. Reluctantly, I met his gaze. My hands were damp with nervous sweat, and my heart thumped so hard in my chest I was sure he could hear its wild patter.

"That was quite a speech, Rocco. But you don't look so happy to see us," he said smoothly. "Why is that? I wonder. Could it have something to do with you thinking you're better than us, now that you're living in Greenwich Village with a rich Irishman?"

He laughed as he saw my look of surprise. "Oh yes, we know all about it."

"How did you escape from the House of Refuge and end up there?" put in Carlo, breathing stale onion breath on me.

"It—it just happened that way. It's only f-for a little while," I stammered. "The blacksmith took me in during the blizzard when . . . when I got away from Randall's Island."

"That was weeks ago. You should know by now where to find us. That very first day, I told you I was the Prince of Bandits' Roost." Tony stepped back and folded his arms. "So, you got yourself arrested and put me and Carlo—your own mob—in danger."

"I never told anyone your names, I swear. I never squealed!"

"Well, don't worry, Rocco," Tony purred. "Everything might still work out just fine. You might even have a chance to make amends for the strain you've caused, what with Carlo and me being so concerned about your welfare and wondering whether you'd turn us in."

"Make amends?"

"I hear Mick Hallanan has done well for himself," Tony went on. "Word is he's quite a sharp businessman."

Tony looked over my head at Carlo. "Wouldn't you think a man like that keeps some ready money at hand, Carlo?"

"I most certainly would," replied Carlo enthusiastically. "I expect the Greenwich Village Blacksmith gets paid every week for the horses he boards there, to say nothing of the money the shoeing operation takes in. Why, I'd guess there are *quite* a number of bank deposits required in an operation like that."

Tony nodded, not taking his eyes off me. "And who is better placed for an inside job than our very own Rocco?"

I tried to smile. Tony himself had taught me that a confident grin can hide uncertainty or confusion; it can buy time to think. And I definitely had thoughts swirling around in my head as wild and furious as blizzard snowflakes.

Up to now, I'd never felt that anything, especially my own fate, was in my hands. Papa had sold me to the padrone; Tony and Carlo had offered me the only way I knew to survive. In the House of Refuge, I was told what to do by the warden and guards.

Yet, since that day I'd escaped, something had begun to shift, almost the way winter finally lets go and spring drifts in. Maybe it had been turning around to help Mary rescue the horses, meeting Max and Mr. Riis, making that first speech to the women in the police station, or just having Mr. Hallanan say quietly, "Good job, Rocco." Maybe it had been listening to *Black Beauty*.

Maybe there was another path I hadn't yet imagined. It might not take me back to Calvello, the way I'd dreamed. But maybe, just maybe, I could find another way to make Papa and Mama proud of me again.

"So, what do you say, Rocco?" said Tony, leaning close. His words were friendly enough, but his eyes told a different story. "Remember, we gave you your first dollar. We made you part of our mob and fed you sausages every day. That's worth something to you, isn't it?"

I gulped and nodded. It was true. And even now there was a lot I would do for a sausage. But not this. I couldn't—I wouldn't—do what Tony wanted. I had to find another way.

Making up my mind, I took a breath.

"I *do* want to earn my way back and be part of the mob again if you'll let me," I assured him, hoping my face wouldn't betray the lie. "But I need more time to learn when the next bank deposit will be. I think it will take place when the regular stableboy returns.

"Have no fear," I went on. "I can find out. He trusts me more every day. His stupid, empty-headed daughter depends on me too."

Tony wanted to believe me, I could tell. After all, there might be a lot of money to be had. He touched the tip of his hat, adjusting it to the most flattering angle. "How much longer do you need?"

"In a week, I should know when and where that deposit will take place. I will meet you here next week at this time. We'll go over the plan to make the touch.

"I may need to lie low for a while afterward, though," I added. "I don't want to go back to Randall's Island."

"We can manage that, if you're good as your word on the rest of the scheme," agreed Tony. "Maybe we can get you to Boston or Philadelphia."

"Tony knows people everywhere," Carlo boasted, almost as if he was talking about himself.

We stood silently for a moment while Tony considered my offer. "One week," he said finally. "Come back to Bandits' Roost next week at this time. And we had better be able to trust you."

# CHAPTER 27

*In which much is revealed
and I begin to become unmuddled*

I began to run as soon as I left the alley. I hadn't gone far when I saw them.

It was unmistakably my padrone, Signor Ancarola, his black hair shining, one large hand on the shoulder of the small boy cowering before him. My heart sank. I knew that boy.

Luigi had been small, even when we left Calvello. Now his eyes looked sunken and rimmed by dark shadows. His ribs protruded from his thin shirt. His feet were bare, covered with soot and mud. The scar from Padrone's brand marked his lip like a dark smudge of ink.

I crept closer, keeping out of sight as best I could behind a vendor's wagon piled high with potatoes. I strained to hear what Padrone was saying. Luigi held up an arm as if to ward off a blow.

I didn't have to hear much to guess what was happening. By now it was early evening, and more than likely Luigi hadn't been able to earn his dollar. I noticed he held a triangle in one hand. Did this mean Marco was too weak or sick—or worse—to wheel the harp along with him now?

More than anything, I wanted to rush over and yank Luigi away from Padrone, especially when he reached out to twist Luigi's arm.

Suddenly I couldn't breathe. I began to tremble with rage. I recognized this feeling—it was the way Mary must have felt standing over the dying horse; it was how Jacob Riis described what happened when his dog was killed.

I'd felt this way before once too—on the night Old Biter got away.


I never would have seen a thing. Any other evening, I would have been long gone from Signor Ferri's property, finished with chores and on my way home.

Old Biter was the last donkey to be returned that night. The peasant who'd rented him for the day probably had worked him hard. As I took the rope from the farmer, Old Biter stubbornly planted his feet, refusing to move another inch. Maybe he was waiting for a kind word or a drink of water. I don't know.

But I was tired too. And without thinking, I tugged on his left ear to get him to move. Old Biter whirled, and nipped me hard on my left arm. The sudden pain made me cry out. I dropped the rope and grabbed my arm.

Big mistake. Tired or not, Old Biter kicked up his back heels and sprinted away. I had to chase him halfway down the hill, his hooves clattering as he bolted along the narrow, darkening streets. Signor Ferri, of course, lived at the top of the town.

I finally caught Old Biter twenty minutes later. As I approached Signor Ferri's yard, I could make out voices. I was still out of sight when I heard Signor Ferri growl, "What do you want?"

I stopped in the shadows, Old Biter now quiet beside me.

Signor Ferri was carrying a lantern, and I saw him hang his jacket on a hook just inside the stable door. Then he turned to the girl who stood waiting, wringing her hands. It was Rosa, my sister Anna's friend.

"Speak up, girl. What is it you want?" he repeated, annoyed. He was, after all, a rich, busy man who didn't appreciate being interrupted when his dinner was waiting.

*He thinks I've already finished up and gone home,* I realized. *He doesn't know I'm here.*

Rosa's father had recently died of fever, leaving her mother alone to raise Rosa and her two little brothers. Mama had been baking an extra loaf of bread for them every week since it happened.

"Please, *signore*," I could hear Rosa saying, "my mama begs a few more days to get you the rent. She is taking in laundry and will soon be paid."

"A likely story." Ferri was a tall, well-fleshed man in his late forties. He towered over the girl. "The rent is late. I have already been patient."

Suddenly he reached down and twisted her arm violently. Rosa cried out. She was Anna's age—thirteen. In the lantern light, she looked much younger, a sad, heartbroken girl. Couldn't he see this?

"And now my patience is used up," he spat. "All my other tenants pay on time. No extension. I want the rent by the morning or your mother must find another place to live."

The landlord dropped her arm, grabbed the lantern, and strode off to the house. Rosa darted by me, her face streaming with tears, before I could call her name.

How could he be so unjust?

I crossed the yard and led Old Biter into the shadowy shed, my hands shaking, anger bubbling inside me.

I noticed Signor Ferri's jacket hanging from its hook. One pocket bulged, heavy with coins. Usually he emptied his pockets. Rosa's presence had distracted him.

I settled Old Biter into his stall and gave him fresh water and hay.

That's when I heard a noise.

෧

Now, as I watched Padrone stomp off, I thrust the memory aside. I ran to where Luigi stood, tears staining his cheeks, clanging his little triangle. He gasped when I took his arm.

"Shh," I whispered. "Come with me."

We pushed our way through the crowds and into a narrow alleyway. Luigi reached out to take hold of my shirt with one grubby hand, almost as if he wondered if I was real. "We thought you were dead."

His dark eyes were wide. "Padrone told us so. He said you were dead. We . . . we didn't want to believe it. We hoped you had gone home."

His clothes were little more than rags. He smelled like garbage.

"We? Is Marco still alive?"

"*Sì,* Marco is alive. But . . . but he often coughs," Luigi told me, still holding on to the edge of my shirt. "Padrone sends him out anyway. He plays a triangle now too. Do you remember Giuseppe? He still plays the violin. I like to stand on the same street to hear his music. Padrone doesn't like that because I . . . I sometimes forget to play.

"Rocco, I am not so good at playing music or getting dollars."

I stared into his pinched little face. Poor Luigi. He still wanted to please Padrone, even now. He was trying to bear whatever happened to him the best he could.

I remembered some lines Mary had read from *Black*

*Beauty*. Beauty's friend, a spirited horse called Ginger, has been cruelly treated. When Beauty asks Ginger why she no longer stands up for herself, Ginger tells him: *"Men are strongest, and if they are cruel and have no feeling, there is nothing that we can do, but just bear it—bear it on and on to the end."*

"Luigi, I need to go now, but we'll meet again, I promise. But you must promise me something too. You must not tell anyone—not even Marco—that you've seen me."

I pressed a dollar into his hand. "Take it."

Mr. Hallanan paid me each week, just as he had promised. Maybe I could send that money home someday.

But right now that didn't matter. Because by the time I got to the stable on Barrow Street and the first horse whinnied a greeting, I was well on my way to knowing exactly what I had to do—even if it meant I'd probably never hear Mary read the end of *Black Beauty*.

# CHAPTER 28

*A bandit's plan*

A plan! After all this time, I finally had one. Oh, I know you're probably wanting to remind me that I've said this before and that, in fact, I'd already failed spectacularly with wild, foolish schemes full of moll-buzzing and secret stashes. But, I promise you, this one was different—though perhaps just as dangerous.

I mulled over the details while I brushed horses, mucked out stalls, filled pails of water, and dumped fresh hay into troughs.

I whispered it to Sheridan, running my hands gently over his scars. He listened to every word, his ears alert. Sometimes he made a soft nickering sound, as if he approved.

I was so distracted that, over supper, Mary had to jab me in the ribs with her elbow to ask for the salt.

"You're a million miles away tonight, lad," said the blacksmith. "How was your afternoon with Mr. Riis?"

"It was . . . it was fine."

"Was it a neighborhood you know?" he said casually, reaching for a piece of bread and buttering it.

"A little," I answered. Once again, I got the feeling Mick Hallanan didn't buy the story I'd spun for him. I felt sure he was watching me closely. That he allowed me to eat at the table with them was probably only because of what we had been through together during the blizzard.

I felt ashamed of sitting there, with all those lies between us.

And maybe that's one reason I made the decision I did: I wouldn't tell Mr. Hallanan about my scheme. I glanced at Mary. I couldn't share it with her. I had lied to her just as much. I wouldn't tell Max or Mr. Riis either.

No, I would tell none of my new friends what I planned to do. They had trusted me, given me responsibilities, treated me with respect and kindness.

And what had I done in return? I had lied—lied about everything. I had lied out of shame, but mostly out of fear. I was a coward.

I didn't have Mary's strong heart, or the courage to tell the truth. Would Mary even want to be friends with an escapee from the House of Refuge? After what had happened to him in the past, what would Mr. Riis say if he found out I had stolen a locket? And would Max and Mr. Hallanan give a pickpocket a job?

No, I had to make things right in my own way—even if it meant I never saw any of them again. I would do this alone.

As promised, I met Tony and Carlo at Bandits' Roost the next week. I wanted to make them think I would go along with the idea of robbing Mr. Hallanan. That would be my best chance of ensuring that Mr. Hallanan's money actually got to the bank.

"I've been keeping my eyes and ears open," I announced. "The blacksmith hasn't gone to the bank since the blizzard because of his injured ankle. Usually it's the stableboy's job, and Tim returns tomorrow, but only part-time. So I'll still be there too."

I lowered my voice. "I overheard the blacksmith say he'll send Tim to the bank after his chores are done. Tomorrow afternoon at three o'clock is when we put our scheme into action. He'll be headed to the East River Savings Institution, a bank at Broadway and West Third."

"We'll be keeping Tim in sight, though he won't see us," said Tony. "I think Broadway will be the best place to make our move."

"I agree. Broadway is crowded," said Carlo, nodding enthusiastically. "It's a good place to make a touch."

"What about you, Rocco?" asked Tony.

"I'll still be at the stable," I said. "I'm sure Mr. Hallanan won't trust me to go with Tim. I'll get away tomorrow night and meet you back here at Bandits' Roost and we can divide the plunder."

That's what I proposed. But I had something else entirely in mind. I intended to sneak out of the stable and take the pouch from Tim before Tony and Carlo did. Then I'd get to the bank and deposit the money safely—without being seen by any of them.

Unfortunately, plans don't always go the way you expect.


The next day, Tim and I were in the courtyard when Mr. Hallanan handed Tim a leather pouch. Right away, I ran into a snag.

"Rocco, I'd like you to go to the bank with Tim," the blacksmith instructed.

"I don't need *him* along, sir," protested Tim.

"Well, it's a large deposit. It won't hurt to have you both on the lookout for pickpockets. All right, Rocco?"

"Uh . . . um, yes, sir. Also, if you remember, Mr. Riis asked me to help him today, so I'll go meet him after we're done," I said. "I . . . I might not be back until much later."

Or not at all.

"That's fine. He said you've been quite helpful." Mr. Hallanan nodded. "Just be careful after dark."

I nodded. As I watched, Tim slipped the pouch into his left jacket pocket. We were ready to go.

*Now what?* My mind raced as we walked under the archway of the courtyard I'd first seen that stormy night a few weeks ago.

I'd had it all figured out so perfectly. I'd have to come up with a new idea—fast.


Tim and I set off together from Barrow Street. Or, rather, Tim marched briskly off, leaving me to trot a few steps behind him, trying to keep up.

I didn't catch sight of Tony or Carlo, but I knew they must be nearby. They'd be following and would be surprised to see me walking with Tim. Would Tony now expect me to act as a stall with Carlo, just as we used to do?

It was less than a half mile to Broadway. I wouldn't have much time to prevent my old mob from taking the money. I knew if they got their hands on it, my chances of getting it back were pretty slim.

Luckily, even the side streets were busy on a spring afternoon. As the crowds pressed close against us, I continued to walk slightly behind Tim on his left, on the outside of the sidewalk. When I made my move, I didn't want to be hemmed in.

Tim hadn't said a word to me. To him, I was as annoying and unwanted as a horsefly. The sooner I was gone from Mr. Hallanan's, the better. The stable was *his* domain.

I could feel my heart pounding. My hands were

sweating. I reviewed in my head everything Tony, Carlo, and Pug had ever told me about the secrets of a good touch.

We were less than two blocks from Broadway when I spotted Tony in the distance. He was leaning casually against a building that boasted a large window. Tony and Carlo must have figured out our route and circled around to get ahead. Now they were ready to put their operation into action. And I'd clearly been wrong about one thing: They would make their move before we got to Broadway.

Carlo was probably on his way toward us. He would time it just right—bumping into Tim directly in front of where Tony stood. When Tim tripped, Tony would make the touch as swiftly as the flick of a snake's tongue.

*Now. I have to act now.*

Just then I got my first piece of luck.

Tony had one bad habit: He couldn't resist preening in the mirrored surface of any window he passed. He must not have spotted Tim and me yet, for I saw him turn to look at his reflection. He reached up to adjust the jaunty angle of his bowler hat, taking his eyes off the flowing stream of people coming toward him.

I would only have an instant. It would have to be enough. I leapt into action.


Moving slightly behind Tim, I stuck out my foot, catching him in midstep. Tim faltered, stumbling slightly forward—just as I'd hoped.

In a flash, I was there to steady him—and snatch the pouch from his pocket. Then, before Tim could realize what had happened, I spun around and darted back the way we'd come, crouching low and weaving through the crowd. At the corner, I crossed the street and glanced back once. On my tiptoes, I could just see Carlo at the spot where Tony had been, looking around uncertainly.

I could almost hear Carlo thinking: *Now, where did Tony go?*

I already knew the answer: Tony was coming after me.

Swerving in and out of carts and horses, I followed a zigzag pattern up and down side streets, trying to lose Tony as best I could. I was glad that just yesterday I'd scouted out the neighborhood by the bank. I'd memorized all the streets and knew exactly where I was headed.

Five minutes. Seven minutes. So far, so good. I was only a block or so from Broadway. Once I got around the next corner, the bank would be in front of me.

I felt someone grab my arm. I whirled, prepared to fight.

"What are you doing, Rocco?" Mary demanded, her eyes blazing. "Where are you going with Da's money?"

Her cheeks were flushed bright red from running—and from anger too.

My mouth dropped open. "What are you doing here?"

"I saw! I was just coming home from school when you and Tim left. I was going to walk with you, but before I could call out, I spotted these two boys watching you. At first, they were following you. Then I saw them put their heads together. Then they took off separately—fast—like they were trying to get ahead and wait for you. They looked so suspicious I decided to follow you. And then I saw what happened—I saw you steal it."

She held out her hand, still breathing hard. "Give me the deposit bag."

"I can't," I cried, shaking my head, all the while scanning the street for Tony. "I'm *not* stealing it. I'm trying to keep it from being stolen. You're right about those boys. And if I give it to you now, they'll get it for sure."

"I'm not stupid!" she snorted. "I bet you're one of them. Da told me he thinks you escaped from the House of Refuge."

So he *had* guessed.

"I did. B-b-but," I stammered, "but it's not what you think. I'm not like that. Not anymore."

"Why should I believe you?"

"I can't make you believe me," I said. I stepped inside a doorway, pulling Mary with me. Still no sign of Tony and Carlo—or Tim either. But it wouldn't be long.

"I know these pickpockets," I told her. "They're good. You need to warn your father to be careful in the future. He can't send Tim by himself anymore. But now . . . right now I have to get to the bank before they do."

I waited. I stuck out my head and spotted a familiar bowler hat turning the corner. "Please, Mary. Please trust me. And, now that you're here, you can help. It's a little dangerous, though."

I figured she wouldn't be able to resist that. And I really did need her. Mary searched my face with her eyes. At last, she let out an exasperated breath. "All right, I'll help. What should I do?"

"One of those pickpockets, the one with the brown bowler, is heading this way. Stay here and pretend to tie your shoe. When he gets to you, stick out your foot and trip him." I thrust out my leg to show her.

"But—and this is important—don't talk to him. And don't try to arrest him or anything!" Knowing Mary, she might want to do just that. "Run the opposite way and come to the bank. I'll leave the deposit receipt for you. You can show your father he was right to trust me."

Mary nodded. "I'll do it. Now go."

She gave me a push.

I took off. As I ran, I wished I'd had time to say how sorry I was.

Something else popped into my head too: I wished I knew how the story ended—and if things turned out all right for Black Beauty.


Mary had never flinched at asking annoyed passengers to get down from an omnibus and walk in the slush. She'd stood up to angry cart drivers abusing their horses. Tripping one pickpocket would not be a problem for a girl like Mary Hallanan.

And whatever she did must have worked, because I reached Broadway without seeing any sign of Tony. Suddenly there it was: the East River Savings Institution, a large, imposing bank with four huge columns in front.

I dashed for the door, almost running down a lady with a big black umbrella. She shook it at me. "Watch out, you ruffian!"

I skidded inside with a little screech and almost fell on the polished marble floor. It was so slippery it was like walking on ice. I wouldn't feel safe until Mr. Hallanan's money was out of my pocket—and in his bank account.

As I made my way across the gleaming floor, a bulky guard appeared, blocking my way.

"May I help you?" he barked, peering down at me with a stern expression.

I straightened my shoulders and pushed back my cap.

"Yes, sir. I'm . . ." I stopped to catch my breath. I practiced my best House of Refuge manners, even remembering to smile. "I'm here to make a deposit for my new employer. I've not been here before. Could you . . . could you please help me?"

"Well, you must be an industrious lad. You look as if you ran all the way here," said the guard, his face softening. "And polite too. I wish I could get my sons to remember to say 'please'! For a minute there, I thought you might be one of those pickpockets who come in here to scout our customers."

He pointed. "Just wait there and a clerk will call you."

"Thank you for your assistance, sir," I said. Warden Sage, I felt sure, would approve.

When it was my turn, I drew the pouch out from inside my shirt. *Whew!* Part of me could hardly believe, even now, that I'd made it.

"Everything all right?" asked the clerk.

"Um . . . yes." My heart was still pounding. "It's just that these days you can't be too careful about pickpockets."

"Oh, don't I know it!" The clerk pulled the full pouch toward him. "I hear stories all the time. Lads as young as you think nothing of stealing from hardworking men— women too. Can you imagine that? What kind of coward would steal from a girl?"

My face must have turned as red as one of George's tomatoes. I waited silently as he counted the bills and coins. Finally, he slipped the money into his drawer and began to write out a receipt.

"Sir, I wonder if I might leave that for someone else to collect," I mumbled. "I . . . I have a further errand, and my employer is sending his daughter here to be sure the deposit has been made."

"Very good. I can put it in an envelope and you can write her name on it. She can ask at any window and we'll see that she gets it."

I hesitated a moment. I had seen Mary's first name on the inside cover of *Black Beauty*. I had been living under the blacksmith's sign. I hadn't done any writing since practicing my letters at the House of Refuge. But now I picked up the pen and wrote, very carefully: *Mary Hallanan.*

# CHAPTER 29

*In which the plan continues
to unfold in breathtaking fashion*

The money was safe. Now I had to keep my appointment with Jacob Riis. He'd told me to meet him at the police reporters' office across from the Mulberry Street police station. I just needed to melt into the crowds and run there without Tony or Carlo catching me. I was pretty sure they wouldn't be very happy with how things had turned out.

Lucky for me, I didn't have far to go.

"Ah, Rocco," said Mr. Riis when I stumbled into his office from the street, red-faced and breathing hard. "You didn't need to run. There's no rush. Our work will just take us to a tenement on Mulberry Bend."

"Yes, sir," I said, still panting.

I didn't have the money any longer, but that didn't mean I was out of Tony's grasp. For now, at least, I was safe with Mr. Riis.

We walked toward Mulberry Bend, where we came to a dim, dreary-looking place called Baxter Street Alley. It was empty except for two girls carrying firewood up and down a wooden stairway. They reminded me of Luigi, with their little faces pinched with hunger.

"Children should be able to play on green grass," Mr. Riis murmured as he set up his equipment.

I asked the girls if Mr. Riis might take their photograph. He set up his tripod and readied the camera. The hard part was setting off the flash powder and timing it so that it ignited just as the picture was taken.

I watched carefully, reviewing the steps in my mind. I would be doing this myself in a very short while.

We worked until just after nightfall. Still no sign of Tony. Probably he was searching in Greenwich Village. I figured the last place he'd expect to find me would be his own neighborhood.

*So far, so good—again.* I was beginning to feel I could actually pull off my entire scheme just as I'd imagined it in Sheridan's stall.

When we returned to the reporters' office, Mr. Riis put his equipment down. Then he removed the exposed plates and loaded the camera with new ones.

"I like to have it all ready for next time," he said. He stretched and took off his glasses to wipe them with his

241

handkerchief. "Rocco, I need to walk over and talk to the sergeant at the station about a story I'm working on. Would you mind watching the equipment until I get back? If you need to leave, just lock the door from the inside."

I nodded. "I'd be happy to."

As soon as he closed the door, I pulled open the top drawer of his desk, grabbed the key I knew would be there, and slipped it into my pocket. I would need it later.

Then I swept up all the equipment—the camera, the tripod, the flash gun, and a bag with the flash powder. I also tucked some matches into my pocket. It was awkward carrying everything, but I only had four or five blocks to my destination.

Locking the door from the inside, I slipped out.


We have now come to the most dangerous but also the most important part of my plan. Because I knew Jacob Riis was right: Without physical evidence, no one would see—or believe.

Balancing the flash gun against a wall, I hid myself at the corner in the shadows near 45 Crosby Street. I was relying on the fact that Luigi never got back to the den early.

I didn't have to wait long. He was alone, dragging his bare feet, probably the last boy in. I could tell by the hopeless set of his shoulders that he hadn't gotten his full dollar.

I reached out and pulled him into my corner.

"Rocco! You came back."

"I told you I would, Luigi. And I need you to do something that might be very hard for you," I whispered urgently. "But Marco's life depends on it. Yours too. Will you help me?"

Luigi nodded. "I will! You've always helped me, Rocco."

"I . . . I'm afraid I haven't been very nice to you, Luigi. I'm sorry."

"You gave me a whole dollar last time we met," Luigi said simply, as if that made up for all the times I'd ignored Marco and him.

I gave him another dollar and told him my plan. I did another thing too: I told Luigi exactly where to find my secret stash under the brick in the alley. It might be the last help I could give him.


I waited alone for an hour, until I was sure everyone in the rear part of 45 Crosby Street had gone to sleep. No flicker of a gas lamp was visible when I slipped around to the back. I flicked a tiny pebble at a cellar window, then went to stand silently by the door.

I wished the windows to the cellar were large enough to fit me and the camera, but they were much too small. That meant I had to rely on the exhausted Luigi to stay awake and be brave enough to creep up the stairs and unlock the door for me from the inside. And that would be the hardest part for little Luigi—not falling asleep after a long day on the streets.

I waited—and waited. Just as I was about to throw another pebble, I heard a slight sound and a fumbling.

Luigi opened the door. We smiled at one another, like brothers with our matching scars.

We tiptoed down the cellar steps. It was exactly as I remembered—the damp, cold walls, the awful smell of unwashed bodies and grime, the chill that seeped into our bones.

For a minute, I felt a ball of panic rise up within me. What would happen if I got caught? Not only would Mr. Riis lose his valuable equipment, but I'd be beaten and locked in here. I couldn't count on being able to escape again.

"*Grazie,* now lie down and close your eyes. Be very still and don't make a sound, no matter what," I told Luigi in a whisper.

I set up the tripod at the foot of the stairs so I could leave quickly. In the dim light of the cellar windows, I could see the boys huddled together on the straw. Still no blankets. My hands were shaking as I sprinkled the powder and got out the matches. I lined up the shot just as carefully as I'd seen Mr. Riis do.

He had taken photographs of boys sleeping before, curled up together in the corners of alleys, curled up around barrels or steam vents or stairs.

This, though, was a picture he'd never have been able to get. No padrone would have let him in. Rooms like this were unknown to any outsider. I felt sure even other immigrants from Italy—like the man with the sausage

I'd met that first day—had no idea just how bad things were here.

I'd found out by working with Mr. Riis that many immigrants lived in terrible poverty, in awful tenement buildings that landlords couldn't be bothered to fix. But these boys didn't go hungry because their whole family was struggling to eke out a living. These boys went hungry because their master didn't want to spend an extra penny on food for them.

It was wrong. And it needed to be stopped, just the way Mr. Bergh and Mary had made the people get off that crowded omnibus.

Only someone who knew what this life was like and that this den existed could take this shot. This was my picture.

What would the boys do when their room suddenly filled with light for a few seconds? I didn't know. I could only hope most were so tired the light would become part of their dreams.

Miraculously, it worked. A few boys stirred and moaned when the flash lit up the room. In one corner, I heard a rat squeak in dismay and scuttle away. I packed up quickly. Before I left, I tucked my shoes under Luigi, who looked up at me sleepily with a faint smile. I took off my cap and put it on Marco's dark hair.

Grabbing the equipment, with the cold, filthy floor under my bare feet, I climbed the stairs to the street.

~

I hung in the shadows of an alleyway until the street outside the reporters' office was empty. Then I ran over, unlocked the door, and made my way in, bulky equipment and all. A gas lamp on the street gave some light, and I carefully put everything back where Mr. Riis kept it.

*Mr. Riis is probably so angry and disappointed in me because he came back and found his equipment gone. I'm sure he thinks I stole everything,* I thought. But that couldn't be helped. Tomorrow he would find out why.

I sat in Mr. Riis's chair. There was a pencil and a reporter's notebook on the desk and just enough light to see. I concentrated hard as I wrote my first letter in English.

*Dear Mr. Riis and Max,*
   *I am sorry I took the camera.*
   *Here is a glass plate. I hope the picture will come out.*
   *The picture shows a secret place.*

I stopped to shake my wrist. Holding the pencil so hard made my hand hurt.

I thought a minute. Mr. Riis kept careful records of where he took pictures, and often these became the captions for his photographs. The first one I helped him with was called, simply, *Elizabeth Street Station—Women Lodgers.*

What should this one be named? Bending to the paper again, I kept writing.

*I think a good title for the picture would be: Child Den, 45 Crosby Street, where a padrone keeps boy street musicians like slaves.*

Then I finished my letter this way:

*I am sorry I lied about everything. I am going to try to make it right.*

> *Rocco*

I left the office without being seen. I'd lost track of time, but thought it must be close to midnight. I shivered. I didn't have a jacket. It was only early April, and a chill breeze caught at my shirt. I felt a few drops of rain. A storm was coming.

"I just hope it's not another blizzard," I mumbled to myself. I wasn't sure I had the courage to go ahead with the rest of my plan if it involved *snow.*

I was glad for the darkness, though it didn't mean I was out of danger. I turned my steps back toward Broadway. I'd head uptown now. I could follow Broadway for blocks and blocks. It might take me an hour of walking to get to Central Park, but even with bare feet, nothing would be as hard as the day I'd escaped from Randall's Island.

Then I came around a corner and walked straight into the Prince of Bandits' Roost.

# CHAPTER 30

*What I owe the donkey; Saint Rocco and me*

Now, as you will recall from the beginning of this tale, I blame the start of my troubles on that bad-tempered donkey. But if there's one thing I've found in all my muddled wanderings, it's that we learn from our misfortunes just as much as from the good things that happen to us.

I cannot tell you exactly why, at this crucial moment, I should suddenly have thought about Old Biter again. Maybe it happened because as soon as Tony saw me, he grabbed hold of my left ear.

"Ouch!" I cried.

And at that moment, I had what you might call an insight into what had happened so long ago. And I realized that perhaps everything hadn't been the donkey's fault. I, too, was to blame.

You see, there are some things about donkey behavior that are well known. Donkeys will not back down if they are threatened. Nor do they like their ears being mishandled. After all, those ears are rather long. No wonder they're sensitive.

So, like the rest of us, donkeys get grumpy when they're annoyed. And when Old Biter got grumpy, he did what came most natural to him: he bit.

And what had I done that night in the landlord's yard? Impatient with the stubborn beast, I had thoughtlessly (and stupidly) pulled on Old Biter's ear to get him to move.

I deserved what I got: a stern warning—and a firm, hard bite.

Now Tony pushed me against a building and pulled my ear again.

"You little liar. We had a deal. You were going to get us the blacksmith's cash," he hissed.

He pinched my ear hard. "That's what you promised."

I gulped. *How am I going to get out of this?*

"Well, what do you have to say for yourself, Rocco?" Tony's mouth was so close I could see his jagged tooth. "Have you forgotten all those days when I fed you, all the things that I taught you? I thought you were one of us."

I was silent. I wasn't trying to be obstinate on purpose. I just had no idea what to say. I had no idea what to do.

"I thought you could be trusted," Tony said. "I was wrong about you, Rocco."

The words sounded familiar. Signor Ferri had said much the same thing.

"The thing is, Tony," I said at last, swallowing hard, "I never really was a pickpocket."

Yes, I had seen Signor Ferri's jacket hanging that night, his pocket bulging with cash. But I had passed it by. And then I had heard that noise.

It was Rosa, fumbling with the landlord's jacket.

"What are you doing?"

She turned around, her face desperate. Signor Ferri's money pouch was in her hand.

Her dark eyes fixed on mine. "Rocco, please."

We stood still.

Then, and I swear this is absolutely true, I felt a gentle nudge, pushing me toward Rosa.

I turned my head, astonished, but Old Biter appeared to be innocently dipping his head to pick up a mouthful of hay.

"Take the money—but give me the pouch. And go," I whispered then, holding out my hand and moving toward her. "I'll take the blame. You have my word: I will tell no one."

And I never had, even when my act brought shame to Papa, even when it led to my banishment. Like Saint Rocco, I allowed myself to be falsely accused.

Signor Ferri was so enraged that I'd taken his money that he forgot about Rosa and her mother. He never connected the theft to her.

And I made sure it was easy to blame me. I let myself be discovered the next day holding the evidence: the empty pouch.

Looking back, I wonder if I could have done it differently. Maybe, if my heart had been as strong as Mary's, I could have stood up to him. I could have raised my voice. I could have changed things.

I would try to change them now.


Tony leaned over and pinched my ear even harder.

I cried out. And then, suddenly as angry as my old friend had been, I reacted. I bit Tony on his arm so hard he screeched and stumbled back in pain. He reached up to punch me, but I was already free, ducking and pushing past him as hard as I could go.

I'd lost track of how many times I had run today—of how long I'd been running from my padrone, from the House of Refuge, from the pickpockets I once knew, from the burden of the secret I had promised to keep for Rosa.

The only people I *wasn't* running away from now were the meddlers of this great city.

This time I was running toward them.

# CHAPTER 31

*In which, at last, I put everything right
and the history approaches its end*

$B$y the time I got to Central Park, it had begun to rain hard. I pushed as far as I could under a bush—but there wasn't much shelter. Trees and shrubs were just beginning to leaf out. I shivered. I was already missing Tim's cot in the stable.

As I'd trudged along, block by block, I'd repeated the same words: "The other half. The other half."

Jacob Riis had explained his work through an old saying: "One half of the world doesn't know how the other half lives."

He wanted to change that. And now, so did I. The other half of the world needed to see—to know about boys like Luigi, Marco, Giuseppe, and the rest. Neighbors in the tenements tried to help one another, I knew that. But so many were struggling just to live and feed their own families. As the man with the sausage had warned me that first day, no one in Little Italy would question the authority of a padrone like Signor Ancarola, just as no one in Calvello had questioned Signor Ferri.

But maybe I could bring the story outside Crosby Street and into the pages of the newspapers. Maybe Max and Mr. Riis would tell the story of a runaway and use my photograph so people could see how boys like Luigi and Marco lived. It was the only way I could think of to try to make things right—even though it meant giving up my freedom.

No. To get people to pay attention, I had to bring the story of boys like Luigi and Marco (and me) to the outside world, just the way Jacob Riis was trying to do. That was why I had come to Central Park as a runaway, and why I intended to stay here until someone found me.

And maybe, just maybe, the plight of one lone, bedraggled boy might be—what was the word I'd heard Max use sometimes? Newsworthy. It might be worthy of a story, and capture people's attention in a way that crowds of poor children did not.

I was doing this the hard way, I knew. I could have told Max and Mr. Riis the truth about my life and asked them to write the story, and use the picture I took with it. Why didn't I? I was embarrassed. I was ashamed too, about how long I had lied to them and to Mary and her father.

No, it was time to start again from the beginning and atone for all the wrong I had done. I had deceived Officer Reilly and run away. I had stolen from people. I had let Luigi and Marco down. I wanted to do something right—for Papa and Mama, and Saint Rocco. And me.

There was something else too.

In my heart, I knew this had to be a real story. I hoped (and it was just a hope) that whoever *did* find me would be shocked—and would want to speak out and tell the world. I wanted to show people the truth the same way Mary and Mr. Bergh had tried to get riders to see how horses suffered in a storm.

And then once the story broke, I knew Max and Mr. Riis would keep on writing, would publish the picture I had taken, and would try to make it right.

That, at least, was my plan.

By the second day, I was hungry and very thirsty. I wandered up and down the park's pathways, not trying to hide myself from passersby. It seemed strange that after working so hard to get free from the House of Refuge, now I was waiting to be caught.

Then, the next morning, I woke to see a man with a shovel peering at me as I lay curled up under a bush. I was covered with dirt. I hadn't slept much because of the cold drizzle.

"Hello there. Don't be scared," said the man in a soft voice, as if he was talking to a skittish colt.

I stared at him and shivered.

"Um . . . do you speak English, boy?" He reached into

a knapsack and held out a roll. I grabbed it with both hands and tore into it hungrily. I didn't have to fake being hungry.

"*Sì,* I speak English. I ran away from a bad padrone," I said hoarsely. "I am a street musician. I am made to play a triangle for money. If I don't get a dollar, I am beaten."

I saw the horror on his face.

"Help me, please. I am scared to go back to Forty-Five Crosby Street."

"I'll take you to my boss," said the man. "He'll know what to do."

That was the beginning. As I would later learn, in the next few days, the story broke in all the newspapers. An ambitious young reporter named Max Fischel, with the help of the increasingly well-known photojournalist Jacob Riis, wrote of boys kept like slaves in a cellar at 45 Crosby Street. There was even a horrifying photograph to accompany the story—a photograph that was, I might add, in perfect focus.

The *New York Times* picked it up under the headline CHILDREN AS SLAVES. In part, the article told how "young Italian children are now suffering the greatest cruelties at the hands of task-masters, or owners, who . . . cruelly and maliciously beat and ill-treat them daily should they not bring home enough money every night to satisfy their greed."

The paper described how the only food served was a three-inch square of black bread and how the children were sent out in all weather. Each child was told "not to come home without having at least a dollar to give the padrone, and if he was not successful enough to be able to hand over so much, after staying out until sometimes after midnight, he was cruelly beaten and tortured to make him say if he had spent any pennies during the day."

Of course, there was a second part of the story, which didn't make the newspaper. Once the authorities had my name, it didn't take them long to figure out I wasn't just an innocent street musician.

Officer Reilly showed up to escort me back to the House of Refuge. He shook his head when he saw me. "I should be mad as a hornet at you, young Rocco. But to be honest, I'm just glad to see you're alive."

"I'm sorry, Officer Reilly. I really am."

He patted my shoulder and handed me a lemon drop. "Come on. I've got the launch waiting. And wasn't that blizzard something? You can tell me all about your adventures on the way back."

One Sunday a couple of weeks later, I got word that I had two visitors. I was led to the visitors' room at the House of Refuge to find Max and Mary waiting for me.

It was all I could do not to cry. I was too embarrassed to look them in the eye. We sat awkwardly in chairs with a table between us.

"Mary's father wanted to join us, but he's home catching up with things. And Mr. Riis is home with his family. But they both send their best wishes," began Max. "They'll be up to see you soon. Mr. Hallanan says to tell you he didn't realize how much work you were doing until you disappeared."

"Thanks." I snuck a glance at Mary, but she wasn't smiling.

"So, how are they treating you?" Max leaned forward and spoke in a low voice. He glanced at the door as if he expected a guard might burst in at any moment.

"They've been . . . fine. Better than I expected," I admitted. And it was true. "Officer Reilly, well, he was so worried about me in the blizzard, he says, he almost had a heart attack. Warden Sage gave me a long lecture about telling the truth."

"You could have told *us* the truth too, Rocco. The whole truth," said Max, banging a hand on the table. "You didn't have to take it all on yourself. We would've helped. Mr. Riis was so worried. We all were. Weren't we, Mary?"

She sat there looking stern. *It would be better if she yelled,* I thought.

"I'm sorry. B-but . . . I—I had to do it this way," I stammered. "I couldn't face you because of all the lies I'd told. It seemed the only way to put everything right—and make people really *see*. Besides, Max, I kept thinking about you being a reporter. You got a better story this way."

"That's true." Max grinned. "About that. I have some good news for you. Mr. Riis was so impressed with your photograph that he's forgiven you for taking his camera the way you did. And the organization Henry Bergh helped to start, the New York Society for the Prevention of Cruelty to Children, is working to convict your padrone. He'll soon be in jail."

"What about the boys at Crosby Street?"

"Officials have contacted relatives, and some of the boys have already gone home," Max told me. "Though I heard of one who can play the violin so well he's been given a scholarship to study music here."

*Giuseppe!*

"Those boys know they have you to thank, Rocco," Max continued. "You allowed yourself to get caught, knowing you'd be sent back here to the House of Refuge."

I flushed and glanced at Mary, who still said nothing. *What is she thinking? If she never wants to talk to me again, why did she come?*

"I'm learning more English and how to write better," I told Max. "I'm in the printshop. That's where I was, uh, before. I'm getting better at typesetting, and now I'm even learning to write stories too—just like you, Max."

"That's good," he said, getting up. "You're going to need those skills."

"What do you mean?"

"When you get out, my newspaper is prepared to offer you a position as a messenger boy, under my direction, of course," he said. "That's how I started, you know. And with a good word from Jacob Riis, I think there's a chance our appeal for you to be released early will be granted."

I stammered my thanks. Maybe I wouldn't spend my thirteenth birthday locked up after all.

"I'll leave you two for a minute," said Max. "I need to speak with the warden."

Now I was in for it.

Mary and I were silent for a time. Finally, I got up my courage.

"I lied to you," I said. "I lied a lot."

"Yes, you did."

"And you're right to be angry. I'm sorry."

I took a breath. "Another thing. It was me, that day. I was the boy who spat at you in the snow last year. I wanted to tell you that."

"I knew that. You looked familiar somehow, then it came back to me when Da asked you about your scar," Mary said. "After that, I just kept waiting to see if you'd say something." She paused. "I thought I was your friend, Rocco. And friends don't lie to each other."

"I know. I guess I'm not very good at being a friend," I told her. "I'd like to get better at it, though."

That much was true. Pug, Jimmy, and George were still here in the House of Refuge. Pug, I knew, would never forgive me, and George would do whatever Pug ordered. But Jimmy and I had begun to at least say hello to one another.

"I'd like to be your friend, Mary Hallanan."

"Okay." Mary began to laugh. "I tried, but I knew I couldn't be mad for long, especially after you helped me in the storm. Besides, I do remember that the first time we met, I hit you pretty hard with those snowballs!"

She pushed a package wrapped in brown paper across the table. "Go on. You can open it."

"For me?"

"You left before I finished the story," she said. "I thought you might want to know what happens in the end."

*Black Beauty!* I ran my hand over the cover of the book.

"I don't know what to say."

She tossed her head, making her braid fly. "You don't have to say anything. But you'd better read the whole book, all the way to the end. Then, when you get out of here, you can read it to *me*."

"All right." I grinned. "Though I'm not sure there'll be time."

"Why not?"

"We might . . . ," I told her, "we might be too busy being meddlers."

"I don't know about you, Rocco Zaccaro," declared Mary Hallanan, "but I will never, ever be too busy to read *Black Beauty*."

# EPILOGUE

## *Spring 1889*

*Giving a delightful account of a parade, as well as some unexpected events that provide a satisfying and heartwarming conclusion to the tale*

M$_y$ story began with a donkey, but it ends with a horse. Lots of horses.

The spring of 1889 was one of the prettiest ever. The sun was so bright that people couldn't help smiling; horses picked up their feet as if dancing through the streets.

Mary was still in school, and still volunteering for the American Society for the Prevention of Cruelty to Animals. She was also making a lot of progress in math, and was helping her father with his business more and more, especially since he was so busy finalizing the patent for his new rubber horseshoe pad. I worked for Mick Hallanan a couple of times a week now. He'd bought another building and had room for twenty-four horses. I could count Tim as a friend. And Sheridan, of course.

I had one other friend too. A few months after I was released from the House of Refuge (just in time for my birthday, I might add), I ran into Carlo, who looked much leaner and stronger than I remembered. He greeted me pleasantly, as if our last interactions had never occurred.

"Tony took a fall, Rocco. He's at the House of Refuge," he said. "You must have just missed him."

I was glad for that. Tony would have made my life miserable. "What about you, Carlo? Are you still . . . you know?"

"Naw." He shook his head. "I'm done with that. I decided if it could happen to a wire as good as Tony, I'd be next. I got a job at the harbor, unloading ships. It's hard work. But you know what? My mother is real proud of me now. And I've got myself a girlfriend too."


It turned out that I'd worked for Mick Hallanan twenty-two days, beginning with the Great Blizzard. Despite the fact that I'd lied to him (quite a lot, if you recall), the blacksmith had paid me for each one. I'd given two of those dollars to Luigi, but I kept the other twenty—the same amount the padrone had promised my family each year. Max had helped me figure out how to send it home to Calvello.

I had three jobs now, which Max and Mr. Hallanan

said meant I was definitely becoming an American. "Americans love to work," they both liked to say about their adopted country.

I read every newspaper I could get my hands on too. I was taking to heart Max Fischel's advice that to be a good reporter, one has to know the news: not just the news from your own paper, but from rival papers too.

That's how I discovered that the first harness parade had been held in London, England, in 1886, as a way to show pride in horses and how crucial it was to treat them kindly.

Now, led by the ASPCA and Mick Hallanan, New York City was holding one of our own. Mary and I got to march down Fifth Avenue at the very head of it, holding a banner reading: WORKHORSE PARADE OF NEW YORK CITY.

There was a grandstand of distinguished and important people; the best horses were awarded fine, shiny ribbons. More than a thousand drivers participated. We had a fair bit of waiting around in Washington Square that morning before we got started. But, I can tell you, I felt a surge of pride as we marched.

As Mary and I set out, the clattering of hooves in our ears, someone waved and shouted, "Rocco! Rocco Zaccaro!"

I laughed, and my sister Anna ran out to plant a kiss on my cheek.

∾

Yes, Anna had come to America. We hoped to bring the rest of the family before too long, what with my earnings and Anna's from her job in a shirtwaist factory. We rented rooms on Elizabeth Street from another family from Calvello. The best part? Signora Marinello's sausages were almost as delicious as the ones Mama made.

It had taken a long time to get Anna here. With help from our priest back home, Anna had been writing simple letters to me ever since my money had reached them. She kept urging me to fulfill my promise to her.

But it wasn't until I saved enough money to buy her passage—and she arrived in New York—that I heard exactly what happened after Luigi and Marco arrived safely home.

"One day, Luigi and Marco and their parents paid us a visit," Anna told me. "It was like a procession. They had gifts and had come to thank Papa and Mama. We gathered outside our doorway, and Luigi made a big speech about how you saved them."

I grinned, remembering how Luigi had made himself stay awake to open the door for me. "He was brave too."

"That's not all," Anna went on. "Rosa's mother came to see Mama and Papa too. She said that you had done a great service to their family."

"She didn't tell them what happened, did she?" I didn't want Rosa to get into trouble.

Anna shook her head. "No, but Papa guessed, because the day before I left Calvello, he brought me to the piazza. Everyone was there, including the landlord.

First, the fathers of Luigi and Marco told everyone that thanks to you, the padrone would go to jail.

"Papa spoke next. He told everyone he was entrusting me, his elder daughter, to you in America. 'My son Rocco has made me proud,' Papa declared."

I flushed. "He said that?"

She nodded. "I wish you'd been there, Rocco."

"That's all right," I told her. "Papa can tell me himself when he joins us."

For the truth was, I no longer dreamed of going home to Calvello. This was my home.

Now, before this history draws to a close, I should tell you how it came to be. Jacob Riis first gave me the idea to put my story on paper.

"So much has happened to you, Rocco," he said one evening as we were heading out to take more photographs. I was, under his direction, becoming a rather good photographer myself. "You should write it down."

"You mean, an autobiography?"

"Exactly," he replied. "I'm hoping to turn my own history into a book one day. I've already decided to include the story of my dog."

"Do you know what you'll call it?"

"Yes. I will entitle it *The Making of an American*." He paused. "What about you?"

I didn't think something so grand would fit my checkered, muddled story. All at once it came to me. "I know! I'll call it *A Bandit's Tale*."

And so I have.

Rocco's Map
of New York City

Randall's
Island
House
of
Refuge

118th St.

Broadway

Central
Park

Mary's House ⊗
Barrow St.
14th St.
Bleecker St.
Houston St.
⊗ Mulberry St. Police
Broome St.
⊗ The Den
Canal St.
Crosby St.
Mulberry St.
⊗ Bandits' Roost
Wall St.
Castle
Garden

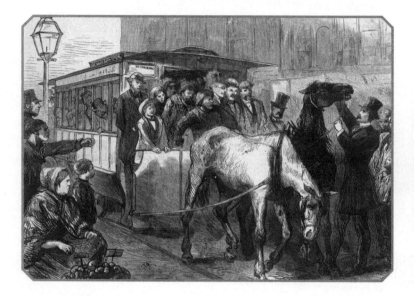

# A NOTE FROM THE AUTHOR

*Containing a variety of facts and resources of possible interest to the reader, as well as information illuminating historical personages*

## A BANDIT'S TALE AND THE PICARESQUE NOVEL

*A Bandit's Tale* is historical fiction written in the style of a picaresque novel. The word "picaresque" comes from the Spanish *pícaro*, which means "rogue" in English. The first picaresque novels were published around 1600 in Spain, beginning a tradition in fiction that continues to this day.

What makes a story picaresque? Most literary critics agree that picaresque novels center on a protagonist who is not wellborn or aristocratic. Instead, like Rocco, the hero is a poor individual forced at a young age to live by his or her wits in an unfriendly or hostile society. The story is often told in the first person and usually has an episodic plot structure—our rogue is an outsider who wanders from misadventure to misadventure, somehow managing to survive. The main character sometimes addresses the reader directly, just as Rocco does. Picaresque heroes are often male, but not always. Perhaps the most celebrated female in the genre is Daniel Defoe's creation Moll Flanders, from his 1722 novel *The Fortunes and Misfortunes of the Famous Moll Flanders.*

Probably the best-known American picaresque novel is *The Adventures of Augie March,* by Saul Bellow, which won the 1954 National Book Award for fiction. It begins: "I am an American, Chicago born—Chicago, that somber city—and go at things as I have taught myself, free-style, and will make the record in my own way." (The observant reader may spot an echo of this opening in Rocco's story.)

One of the masters of the comic picaresque novel was Henry Fielding, author of *The History of Tom Jones, a Foundling* (1749) and *The History of the Adventures of Joseph Andrews, and His Friend Mr. Abraham Adams* (1742). The delightful chapter headings of both novels (which you can read online through Project Gutenberg) inspired those in this book.

The novelist Charles Dickens admired Fielding and even named one of his sons Henry Fielding Dickens. Dickens wrote several of his own novels in a picaresque style, including *Oliver Twist; or, The Parish Boy's Progress* (1838), which inspired the musical *Oliver!,* and *The Life and Adventures of Martin Chuzzlewit* (1844). Dickens used his novels to explore social issues of the day and, as we shall see below, could certainly be considered a "meddler" in his own right.

## THE SETTING

*A Bandit's Tale* takes place in New York City in the late nineteenth century. A time of tremendous change and turmoil, it seemed the ideal setting for a story of an uprooted boy living on the outskirts of the underworld. Through much of the nineteenth century, immigrants from Ireland, Italy, and Eastern Europe crowded into the Lower East Side, peddling on the streets, doing piecework at home, and toiling in the

sweatshops and factories of America's burgeoning industrial revolution. Living conditions for poor families could be brutally harsh; immigrant children often began work at a young age.

Charles Dickens was himself no stranger to hardship. At age twelve, after his father was put into debtors' prison, Dickens lived on his own and worked in a boot-blacking factory. This personal experience may have been part of why Dickens advocated social responsibility in novels such as *A Christmas Carol* (1843).

During his tour of the United States in 1842, Dickens went to Five Points, the heart of New York City's slums. He recorded his impressions in a book commonly referred to as *American Notes:* "This is the place: these narrow ways, diverging to the right and left, and reeking everywhere with dirt and filth. . . . From every corner, as you glance about you in these dark retreats, some figure crawls half-awakened. . . . Where dogs would howl to lie, women, and men, and boys slink off to sleep, forcing the dislodged rats to move away in quest of better lodgings."

Dickens influenced other social reformers of the time, including the pioneering photojournalist Jacob A. Riis. An immigrant to the United States from Denmark, Riis once worked selling subscriptions to Dickens's novels door to door. Later, established as a reporter, Riis used both stories and images to illuminate the lives of the city's poor.

*A Bandit's Tale* takes place during a pivotal time in Riis's career. One day, in the fall of 1887, Riis read a newspaper account of the invention of flash photography. Immediately he realized the impact that photographs could have on the public. Riis taught himself photography and began using it to shed light on the darkest corners of the tenements. (Check out the "Reading and Resources" section for information on how you can see a demonstration of the flash technique and equipment Riis used to take his startling photographs.)

Published in 1890, Riis's groundbreaking work *How the Other Half Lives* is considered the first book to use photojournalism in the battle for social justice. Riis's efforts to expose untenable living conditions for the poor attracted the attention of the future U.S. president Theodore Roosevelt, who in 1895 was named police commissioner of New York City.

Roosevelt became a partner to Riis in his crusade. They championed reforms such as tearing down the notorious tenements in the Five Points neighborhood, establishing parks, and requiring landlords to provide adequate light and sanitation. They also investigated contaminated water supplies, which could lead to cholera, and worked to enact child-labor laws.

In 1897, reflecting on what they had achieved together, Roosevelt told Riis that he had undertaken this work "because I was trying, with much stumbling and ill success, but with genuine effort, to put into practice the principles you had set forth, and to live up to the standard you had established."

## The Rights of Children and Animals

In *A Bandit's Tale,* the fictional characters Rocco and Mary find themselves caught up in two social-reform movements of this time: preventing cruelty to children and improving the treatment of animals. In the mid-1800s in New York City, these were closely linked.

Rocco Zaccaro is a street musician from the town of Calvello in southern Italy. His situation is based on documented examples of Italian padroni bringing children (both boys and girls) from this region to Paris, London, and New York to be street musicians. In New York in the early 1870s, Italian padroni kept children at 45 Crosby Street in conditions much like those described in *A Bandit's Tale.*

In the summer of 1873, one of those boys, named Joseph, ran away to Central Park, where he hid for several days before being discovered. His story, reported in the *New York Times,* helped to raise public awareness. Legislation was passed (the "Padrone Act" of 1874) to stop this exploitation of children. Information in *A Bandit's Tale* on street musicians is based on an excellent scholarly book by John E. Zucchi.

I have taken liberties with the historical dates of this abusive practice. By the time of our tale, in the late 1880s, the practice of children being exploited as street musicians in New York City had mostly been halted. Since flash photography had not been invented when these "child dens" were active, there are no photographs, so far as I know, showing their interiors. Thus, the incident where Rocco takes the camera into his own hands is entirely fictionalized.

The character of Rocco's padrone, Giovanni Ancarola, is based on an actual person. In the fall of 1879, the New York Society for the Prevention of Cruelty to Children was alerted by Italian officials that a man named Antonio Giovanni Ancarola was about to arrive in the United States with seven boys. Soon after, Ancarola was arrested and sentenced to five years in prison. The boys had been indentured for four-year terms, with their parents receiving between sixteen and thirty-two dollars a year.

Readers may wonder if padroni actually scarred the street musicians. A July 22, 1873, *New York Times* article about child street musicians reported that "it has been discovered that but few of the boys are without a brand of some kind by which they can be recognized.

"Many of them wore a diagonal cut on either the right or left side of the upper lip, which has been purposely made and sewed up again in a rough manner, so that the scar will always remain. Others have their under lip split in the centre, and a permanent scar is secured in the same manner. These cuts about the mouth are the most preferable style of brand, because to the casual observer they present nothing unnatural, as the marks may be readily taken as the result of an accident."

The social reformer Henry Bergh, another historical figure who appears in our story, is remembered for his commitment to helping both children and animals. In 1864, after years of witnessing animal cruelty during travels in Europe, Bergh stopped in England to consult with leaders of the Royal Society for the Prevention of Cruelty to Animals, which had been founded in 1824.

Back home in New York, Bergh contacted wealthy people to obtain their support for his Declaration of the Rights of Animals. Thanks to his campaign, the American Society for the Prevention of Cruelty to Animals was established on April 10, 1866. Today we celebrate April as Prevention of Cruelty to Animals Month.

Henry Bergh's success in animal rights led to his involvement in the New York Society for the Prevention of Cruelty to Children. In 1873, Bergh and a lawyer for the ASPCA, Elbridge Gerry, helped to bring attention to the situation of an abused girl known simply as Mary Ellen. When the case went before a judge, Jacob Riis was in the courtroom to write about it. You can read about this landmark case on the ASPCA's website (see the "Reading and Resources" section). Bergh and Gerry subsequently worked to found the New York Society for the Prevention of Cruelty to Children, which was established on April 27, 1875, and served as its vice presidents.

In researching *A Bandit's Tale,* I had the pleasure of visiting that organization's headquarters and viewing some of its first annual reports, which document the successful effort to prosecute Ancarola. I also spent time at the Museum of the City of New York, where I was able to read many letters that Bergh wrote to city officials advocating better roads and water fountains for horses. He was definitely persistent! It's no wonder he earned the nickname the Great Meddler.

In the nineteenth century, horses were primarily thought of as living machines. The plight of workhorses received further attention in 1877, when a British author named Anna Sewell published her only novel, *Black Beauty*. (The novel is available to read free online.) In real life, as in our story, the book was a favorite with readers like Mary Hallanan. It became an immediate success on both sides of the Atlantic.

## HISTORICAL FIGURES AND INSTITUTIONS (AND A PARADE)

While historical figures, institutions, and events make appearances in *A Bandit's Tale,* the book is a work of fiction. When characters speak, their dialogue is invented. Below you will find short biographies of actual people, as well as some brief information on real organizations, that appear in the story.

ANTONIO GIOVANNI ANCAROLA was tried in 1879 by the New York Society for the Prevention of Cruelty to Children, which Henry Bergh helped to establish. While that is fact, I have imagined Ancarola's description, character, and actions in *A Bandit's Tale.*

HENRY BERGH (1813–1888) was born in New York City, the son of a wealthy shipyard owner. After inheriting part of his father's fortune, he and his wife, Matilda, traveled extensively in Europe. He began his crusade for the rights of animals in February 1866 and served as the voice of the ASPCA from its founding in April 1866 until his death twenty-two years later. The man known as the Great Meddler passed away early on the morning of March 12, 1888, in the midst of the Great Blizzard of 1888. (You can read more about this famous storm in Jim Murphy's *Blizzard!;* see the "Reading and Resources" section.)

Bergh's obituary in the *New York Times* relates one incident that helped inspire a scene in *A Bandit's Tale.* During one winter storm, when the slush was ankle-deep, Bergh and some of his followers gathered where several horse-drawn streetcar lines merged. "Henry Bergh gave orders to take from the tracks every horse that had an ailment or a sore. The condition of the wretched animals attached to the cars at that time was notoriously bad."

As a result, the lines virtually shut down, sending passengers into the street. "Thousands of people had to foot it up town in the rain and the slush, growling, cursing, hungry, wet, and mad. 'Who did this?' was the angry question asked on all sides, and to this came but one reply, 'Bergh,' and the public at last discovered that he and his society had developed into a mighty power."

GERARDO FERRI and his wife, Michelina, bought the first piano in Calvello in 1879. It was brought up by mules and became a status symbol for one of the most important land-owning families in the hill town. The character and actions of Signor Ferri in this story are entirely fictionalized, with no relation to the real historical figure or his family.

MAX FISCHEL (1863–1939), a Jewish newspaperman born in Prague, came to America at age four and grew up on Houston Street in New York, near the police headquarters on Mulberry Street mentioned in our story. Called a "natural-born reporter," Fischel got his start in newspaper work as a messenger boy. As he does in *A Bandit's Tale,* Max Fischel served as Riis's guide to Jewish neighborhoods, helping to persuade people to share their stories and have their photographs taken for the first time.

MICHAEL HALLANAN (c. 1847–1926), the Greenwich Village Blacksmith, actually did invent a special rubber horseshoe pad. Hallanan lived near Sheridan Square in Greenwich Village; you can still see his initials on one of the buildings he owned on Barrow Street. In his obituary in the *New York Times,* the blacksmith is also credited with suggesting that the triangle at the intersection of Barrow Street, West Fourth Street, and Washington Place be named in honor of the Civil War cavalry leader General Philip Sheridan. Hallanan came from Galway, Ireland; he died at the age of seventy-nine and was survived by four children, one of them named Mary. The words and actions of Mick Hallanan in this story are imagined.

JACOB A. RIIS (1849–1914) was a Danish immigrant and pioneering American journalist. In 1888, after learning how to take flash pictures, he began gathering photographs and stories for his lectures on the plight of people in the tenements. According to one biographer, while snowbound during the Great Blizzard of 1888, Riis hatched the idea to reach more people by writing a book. He sent in a title description to the U.S. Copyright Office on March 19, 1888. Destined to become one of the most influential books of its time, *How the Other Half Lives* was published in 1890.

Riis's stories about the gold locket and his dog being killed are included in his autobiography, *The Making of an American* (1901), which is available through Project Gutenberg.

The NEW YORK HOUSE OF REFUGE, the first public institution in America to deal with juvenile delinquents, was established in 1825. It also housed orphans. The House of Refuge on Randall's Island opened in 1854. There was a large building for boys, serving several hundred children, and a smaller one for girls. It closed in 1935. While Rocco's escape is imagined, I borrowed from the reports of several (mostly unsuccessful) escapes published through the years in the *New York Times*.

The FIRST WORKHORSE PARADE in New York City, with twelve hundred entries, actually took place in 1907, as part of the effort to improve the treatment of horses. The first parade in London was held in 1886, while Boston was the site of the first U.S. event, in 1903. The tradition continues to this day in England.

## How to Talk Like a Thief

For the details of the pickpocket scenes in this story, I relied on the historian Timothy J. Gilfoyle's *A Pickpocket's Tale: The Underworld of Nineteenth-Century New York,* a study of the pickpocket George Appo. I also took many details from the first-person account of a New York City thief named Jim Caulfield, who was interviewed by the journalist Hutchins Hapgood. Hapgood recorded Caulfield's story of his life of crime in a 1903 book titled *The Autobiography of a Thief*. Here are some phrases straight from the horse's mouth.

**Bang a super:** Steal a man's watch by detaching it from the chain; may also be called "get a man's front"

**Blow:** Take alarm

**Breech-getting:** Picking a man's pocket (as opposed to moll-buzzing)

**Copper:** Policeman

**Dip or Pick:** Person who actually picks someone's pocket; may also be called a "wire"

**Graft/Grafter:** Thievery/Thief

**Hoisting:** Shoplifting

**Leather:** Wallet or pocketbook

**Make a touch:** Pick a pocket

**Moll-buzzing:** Stealing from women

**Mouthpiece:** Lawyer

**Pen or Stir:** Penitentiary/Jail

**Pinched:** Arrested

**Plunder:** Money or stolen object

**Rattler:** Streetcar

**Sneak thief:** Thief who sneaks into houses to steal; a burglar

**Spring/Fall money:** Money set aside to bribe a policeman or pay a lawyer to help "spring" a thief from jail; this savings is sometimes also called "fall money" because it is set aside in the event of a "fall" (arrest)

**Squeal:** Tell on someone

**Stall:** Person who creates a distraction to hide what the dip is doing

**Sucker:** Victim

# READING AND RESOURCES

## BOOKS FOR YOUNG READERS

Bial, Raymond. *Tenement: Immigrant Life on the Lower East Side*. Boston: Houghton Mifflin, 2002.

Freedman, Russell. *Kids at Work: Lewis Hine and the Crusade Against Child Labor*. Photographs by Lewis Hine. New York: Clarion Books, 1994.

Hopkinson, Deborah. *A Boy Called Dickens*. Illustrations by John Hendrix. New York: Schwartz & Wade Books, 2012.

———. *Shutting Out the Sky: Life in the Tenements of New York, 1880–1924*. New York: Orchard Books, 2003.

Kirby, Matthew J. *The Clockwork Three*. New York: Scholastic, 2010.

Loeper, John J. *Crusade for Kindness: Henry Bergh and the ASPCA*. New York: Atheneum, 1991.

Murphy, Jim. *Blizzard! The Storm That Changed America*. New York: Scholastic, 2000.

Napoli, Donna Jo. *The King of Mulberry Street*. New York: Wendy Lamb Books, 2005.

Sewell, Anna. *Black Beauty: The Autobiography of a Horse*. London: Jarrold and Sons, 1877. (Numerous reprint

editions are available, and the book also can be read
through Project Gutenberg.)

ONLINE RESOURCES

"ASCPA April: Prevention of Cruelty to Animals Month,"
ASPCA, aspca.org/get-involved/aspca-april.
"The 1834 Thomas Cox House—No. 17 Barrow Street," blog
entry by Daytonian in Manhattan, daytoninmanhattan
.blogspot.com/2012/11/the-1834-thomas-cox-house-no-17
-barrow.html. This blog includes photos of the building
where Michael Hallanan ran his horseshoeing operation.
"Founding and Early History," New York Society for the
Prevention of Cruelty to Children, nyspcc.org/about
/history.
"Henry Bergh: Angel in Top Hat or the Great Meddler?,"
blog entry by Tammy Kiter, New-York Historical Society
Museum & Library, blog.nyhistory.org/henry-bergh
-angel-in-top-hat-or-the-great-meddler.
"Light," *How We Got to Now with Steven Johnson,* PBS, pbs
.org/how-we-got-to-now/home. This episode includes a
demonstration of techniques of flash photography used
by Jacob Riis.
*The London Harness Horse Parade,* Amazon Instant Video,
amazon.com/The-London-Harness-Horse-Parade
/dp/B004P0UVAK. A documentary of the 2003 event;
shorter videos are available free on YouTube.
"The London Harness Horse Parade," London Harness
Horse Parade Society, lhhp.co.uk.
"Virtual Tour," Lower East Side Tenement Museum,
tenement.org/Virtual_Tour/index_virtual.html.

Alland, Alexander, Sr. *Jacob A. Riis: Photographer and Citizen.* Millerton, New York: Aperture, 1974.

Anbinder, Tyler. *Five Points: The 19th-Century New York City Neighborhood That Invented Tap Dance, Stole Elections, and Became the World's Most Notorious Slum.* New York: Plume, 2002.

Beers, Diane L. *For the Prevention of Cruelty: The History and Legacy of Animal Rights Activism in the United States.* Athens: Ohio University Press / Swallow Press, 2006.

Buk-Swienty, Tom. *The Other Half: The Life of Jacob Riis and the World of Immigrant America.* Translated by Annette Buk-Swienty. New York: W. W. Norton, 2008.

Gilfoyle, Timothy J. *A Pickpocket's Tale: The Underworld of Nineteenth-Century New York.* New York: W. W. Norton, 2006.

Hapgood, Hutchins. *The Autobiography of a Thief.* New York: Fox, Duffield, 1903.

McNeill, J. R. *The Mountains of the Mediterranean World: An Environmental History.* Cambridge: Cambridge University Press, 1992.

McShane, Clay, and Joel A. Tarr. *The Horse in the City: Living Machines in the Nineteenth Century.* Baltimore: Johns Hopkins University Press, 2007.

Riis, Jacob A. *How the Other Half Lives: Studies Among the Tenements of New York.* New York: Charles Scribner's Sons, 1890.

———. *The Making of an American.* New York: Macmillan, 1901.

Tak, Herman. *South Italian Festivals: A Local History of Ritual and Change.* Amsterdam: Amsterdam University Press, 2000.

Zucchi, John E. *The Little Slaves of the Harp: Italian Child Street Musicians in Nineteenth-Century Paris, London, and New York.* Montreal: McGill-Queen's University Press, 1992.

## Source Notes

### Epigraphs

"Long ago it was said . . .": Riis, Jacob, and Luc Sante. *How the Other Half Lives: Studies Among the Tenements of New York*. New York: Penguin Books, 1997. Print 5.

"'Do you know why . . .'": Sewell, Anna. *Black Beauty: The Autobiography of a Horse*. 1877. Project Gutenberg, 16 Jan 2006. n.p. Web. 24 Feb 2015.

"I have counted . . .": Bergh, Henry. Letter. *New York Times*, Dec 26, 1871. Web.

### Chapter 23

"The first place that I can well remember . . .": Sewell, *Black Beauty*, n.p.

### Book Four

"With appetite ground to keenest edge . . .": Riis, *How the Other Half Lives*, 137.

## CHAPTER 27

"Men are strongest . . .": Sewell, *Black Beauty,* n.p.

## CHAPTER 31

". . . young Italian children are now suffering . . .": "Children as Slaves," *New York Times,* June 17, 1873.

". . . not to come home without . . .": Ibid.

## A NOTE FROM THE AUTHOR

"I am an American, Chicago born . . .": Saul Bellow, *The Adventures of Augie March,* with an introduction by Christopher Hitchens (New York: Viking Press, 1953; New York: Penguin Books, 2003), 1.

"This is the place . . .": Charles Dickens, *American Notes for General Circulation and Pictures from Italy* (London: Chapman & Hall, 1913; Project Gutenberg, 1996), n.p.

"'. . . because I was trying . . .'": Buk-Swienty, *The Other Half,* 245.

". . . it has been discovered that . . .": "The Italian Slaves," *New York Times,* July 22, 1873.

"Henry Bergh gave orders . . .": "Death of Henry Bergh," *New York Times,* March 13, 1888.

"Thousands of people had to foot . . .": Ibid.

# PICTURE CREDITS

# ACKNOWLEDGMENTS

I am indebted to Allison Wortche and Katherine Harrison, my editors, for embracing Rocco's story and for helping to bring this tale to life through their perceptive insights and suggestions. Thanks also to Nancy Hinkel and so many people at Alfred A. Knopf and Random House, including Anne Schwartz, Lee Wade, Adrienne Waintraub, Laura Antonacci, Lisa Nadel, Aisha Cloud, Lisa McClatchy, Melanie Cecka, Karen Greenberg, Kate Gartner, Trish Parcell, Iris Broudy, Amy Schroeder, and Lisa Leventer. My agent, Steven Malk, is unfailingly supportive, and Michele Kophs of Provato Marketing is a wizard with social media, blog tours, and websites.

As I often tell students during my author visits, history must be seen. Barbara Noseworthy and Jim Cunningham generously allowed me to stay in their New York City apartment while on a trip to research this book.

*A Bandit's Tale* became a family affair. I'm grateful to my daughter, Rebekah, for accompanying me on several long (and hot) walks during that trip, traipsing around neighborhoods in which Rocco and Mary would have wandered. We tracked down 45 Crosby Street and craned our necks to make out Michael Hallanan's initials on the former site of the blacksmith shop and stable on Barrow Street. I hope that Rebekah's students at the Lake Champlain Waldorf School will enjoy Rocco and Mary's story. My niece Ellie Thomas, who grew up in New York City, was also an integral part of this research trip. My husband, Andrew Thomas, created

Rocco's map and read an early draft of the manuscript, and my son, Dimitri, became the first listener, critiquing as I read the final draft aloud. Even the dogs helped. When Brooklyn and Rue barked, we would go for a walk and I'd think about Rocco's next misadventure.

Thanks to Joseph T. Gleason, director of archives at the New York Society for the Prevention of Cruelty to Children, for his generous assistance and for access to archived annual reports, which chronicle the arrest of Giovanni Ancarola. Thanks also to Lindsay Turley, assistant director of collections at the Museum of the City of New York, for making ASPCA papers and the letters of Henry Bergh available; and to Nilda I. Rivera, the museum's director of licensing and reproductions, for her help in obtaining photographs by Jacob Riis. Any errors of fact or interpretation are my own.

Since becoming a full-time writer in 2014, I have had the privilege of visiting many more schools and of attending conferences across the country. I am so grateful to all the librarians, educators, and parents who champion children's literature and help young people discover a love of reading (and especially reading about history!).

Thanks to my sisters, Janice Fairbrother and Bonnie Johnson, for always being there—they may recognize the twinkling eyes of our dear late father, Russell W. Hopkinson, in Officer Reilly. As always, Deborah Wiles helped me believe I could tell this story. I am fortunate to have wonderful friends, including Vicki Hemphill and family, Elisa Johnston, Ellie Thomas, Teresa Vast and Michael Kieran, Maya Abels, Sheridan Mosher, Kristin Hill and Bill Carrick, Deniz Conger, Cyndi Howard, Deborah Correa, Sara Wright, Becky and Greg Smith, Nick Toth, Eric Sawyer, Kathy Park, and many more. As always, I am grateful to my husband and children for bringing me such love and joy.

# ABOUT THE AUTHOR

DEBORAH HOPKINSON has written more than forty books for young readers. She is the author of the middle-grade novels *Into the Firestorm: A Novel of San Francisco, 1906* and *The Great Trouble: A Mystery of London, the Blue Death, and a Boy Called Eel,* winner of the Oregon Spirit Book Award and cited as a *School Library Journal* Best Book of the Year.

Her picture books include *Sky Boys: How They Built the Empire State Building,* an ALA-ALSC Notable Children's Book and a *Boston Globe–Horn Book* Honor Book; *Abe Lincoln Crosses a Creek,* an ALA-ALSC Notable Children's Book; *A Boy Called Dickens; Annie and Helen;* and *Sweet Clara and the Freedom Quilt,* winner of the International Reading Association Children's Book Award.

Deborah Hopkinson lives with her family in Oregon. Please visit her online at DeborahHopkinson.com.

# Join Deborah Hopkinson on another historical adventure!

★ "A delightful combination of race-against-the-clock medical mystery and outwit-the-bad-guys adventure."
—*Publishers Weekly*, Starred

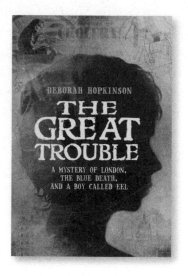